OVERSIGHT

THE COMMUNITY: BOOK II

SANTINO HASSELL

RIPTIDE
PUBLISHING

Riptide Publishing
PO Box 1537
Burnsville, NC 28714
www.riptidepublishing.com

Oversight

Cover art: Kanaxa, kanaxa.com
Editor: Sarah Lyons
Layout: L.C. Chase, lcchase.com/design.htm

ISBN: 978-1-62649-508-1

First edition
June, 2017

Also available in ebook:
ISBN: 978-1-62649-507-4

OVERSIGHT

THE COMMUNITY: BOOK II

SANTINO HASSELL

RIPTIDE
PUBLISHING

For everyone who has the courage to Resist.

TABLE OF
CONTENTS

CHAPTER ONE

There was something about having a six-foot-six bouncer kneeling between his thighs that left an indelible impression on Holden.

In his youth, the big guys had always refused to suck him off. They'd also refused to bend over for him. It would have been fine had the refusals not been tinged with the undeniable odor of disdain for men who enjoyed such acts. Even as a teenager, Holden had not been there for anyone's toxicity or self-loathing fuckery. He was there for sex, not therapy. If he wanted therapy, he'd go to the Community Watch and overshare with Community counselors about his sexual frustrations like so many other people did.

Instead, he'd gravitated to twinks and—back when the term was an accepted part of the gay lexicon—flamers. Men who didn't feel obligated to perform society's version of masculinity. And it'd been fine at first, but he was attracted to many, so why limit himself to a few?

A decade later, all that had changed. The world hadn't run out of toxic self-loathing men, but sexual hang-ups seemed to fall away as people got older, and the millennials seemed to be born without them. Holden's thirties had definitely been more fun than his twenties. People were more willing to go out of their comfort zones, and *that* he was definitely here for. Especially if it came in the form of six-foot-six Vikings.

Not only was the allegedly straight giant more talented than expected with his tongue, but he'd had no hesitations about gracing his boss with some oral attention before Evolution opened for the evening. Holden hadn't needed to soothe overactive hetero nerves with his psychic abilities—Stefen's eagerness had been one hundred percent genuine. Now here he was, proving to the world—or just to Holden—that more men than the general public liked to believe were willing to get on their knees for the right queer.

"Faster," he said, stroking the shiny red hair falling around his thighs. "Take it all the way down."

A muffled sound answered the suggestion.

Holden was glad Stefen couldn't talk. He was a new employee at Evolution, and he hadn't proven to be the brightest bulb in the box they'd been hurriedly trying to fill for the past few months. All it had taken was another big scandal, this one bigger than the others, to clear the Community's only LGBT club of its staff. People were starting to think it was cursed. Or targeted.

In a way, they were right.

When the disappearances had begun, Holden hadn't found a connection between the psys who'd wound up vanishing from his nightclub, but no matter what the rumor mill had claimed about his lack of action . . . he'd tried. Then Theo's apparent suicide had turned his concern into outright terror. In all of their interactions, he'd never sensed the younger man had been a threat to himself. Just Evolution's reputation. Holden's reputation. And by default, his father's and the Community's.

The events leading up to Theo's death had been a storm looming just beyond Evolution's location on Tenth Avenue in Hell's Kitchen, a menacing darkness that had sent unease slithering along Holden's body, but the murder of Theo's boyfriend, Jericho, had sealed it for Holden. There was no denying that something wasn't right with the club after a crowd of club goers had swarmed the Dreadnought's bass player in a sudden homicidal fury. It had to be connected to Theo and the disappearances Theo had been investigating. Yet Holden had never imagined the mastermind behind it all was the woman his own father had sent to watch over him. To make sure *he* wasn't screwing up. What were the odds?

What were the odds.

Coincidences didn't feel good. They didn't look good or smell good. Especially not when he was surrounded by people with extrasensory abilities—people who should have seen her coming. But they hadn't. His own father hadn't.

Holden closed his eyes and tilted his head back. He massaged Stefen's scalp and focused on the wet heat surrounding his dick. It should have been enough to keep his thoughts from wandering down dark paths with unknown end points, but it wasn't. His constant worrying and wondering had kept him awake most nights for the past several months because he had no idea what to expect. As powerful as his gift of empathy was, it did nothing to clue Holden in about what other unfortunate incidents would occur in the future and give the coup de grâce to both Evolution and his position in the Community.

Stefen abruptly pulled off his dick, leaving it glistening with spit. "Are you gonna come?"

"Not even close."

Stefen cocked his head, maybe offended, maybe puzzled, and went back to work. He was so earnest about it, despite the claim that he'd never touched a dick besides his own. That endeared him to Holden. Stefen wasn't worth a damn as a bouncer—too nice, too understanding, too reluctant to turn anyone away—but he was certainly eager to please. Even if he wasn't very good at this either.

Holden petted the bouncer's long red hair and marveled at his ability to be bored by a blowjob. If the recent trauma began to affect his sex life as well as his stress level, it would be time to buckle down and commit himself to seeing a counselor. Not a Community counselor. Those were all located at the Community's headquarters downtown and required members to sign a contract that all their sessions be recorded. The underground psychic community did not believe in HIPAA. They were more invested in ensuring no one was distraught enough to expose the existence of the organization, and psychics in general, to the public.

If there was one thing all members of the Community agreed on, it was that being outed would be disastrous. If outsiders knew about them, they would be harmed. Holden had grown up on that us-against-them verbiage, but there was little evidence that it wasn't true. It was very easy to see how the rest of the world would view them as either tools or threats, and react accordingly.

It took several more minutes for Stefen to find a rhythm. Just as Holden's breathing picked up and he felt the tug of his arousal coiling for release, the office door swung inward. Stefen threw himself backward, his teeth skimming Holden's dick. Holden hissed and covered himself, holding onto his expletives only because his father was now looming in front of him.

Richard Payne took one look at them and turned away. "Get him out of here."

"Jesus." Holden tucked himself into his pants and jerked his head at Stefen. "Go."

"Yeah. I'm going." Stefen staggered to his feet. He wiped his mouth but only managed to look even sloppier and more freshly used. "Sorry, boss."

Holden rubbed his forehead and closed his eyes. "Just . . . leave."

Stefen scuffled out without saying anything to Richard. Either he didn't recognize one of the Community's founders, or he was too embarrassed to care. However, judging from his parting question of whether they wanted the door open or closed, it was entirely possible he was simply an imbecile. Holden fought a smile and opened his eyes.

"That was unfortunate timing."

"Is that what you're calling it?" Richard skimmed his eyes over him, judgment and disdain etched into the ice of his features. They looked very alike, from the tawny hair to the hazel eyes and lean build, but that was where the similarities ended. While Richard never cracked a smile, Holden tried his best to find dark humor in the serious. His father tended to overanalyze and look for weaknesses and problems even in the best of situations, whereas Holden often took things at face value because he'd rather believe things were going well. And last, but definitely not forgotten, was the fact that although they were both empaths, Holden's gift was notably stronger. Nothing like being one-upped by your own son to trigger resentment instead of pride.

Psychics were fucked up.

"What would you like me to call it?" he wondered. "Unfortunately, I didn't inherit Mother's talent for precognition, so I had no idea you would be barging into my office."

"And yet you have a wall of cameras right in front of you," Richard said dryly.

"Touché."

Holden glanced at the cameras in question. The main level of Evolution was empty of all but staff, and the VIP level was cast in the gloom of darker lights. In the past, he'd enjoyed seeing it void of patrons. He'd liked to see the place he'd created in all of its glory before it was desecrated by drunken psys who would inevitably end up puking or fucking at various locations throughout the space. But, now, he wasn't as entranced by the stillness. It gave a spectral vibe that reminded him of another night not too long ago when the empty club had nearly been the setting for yet another murder. His own.

Swallowing the knot in his throat, he crossed his arms over his charcoal suit jacket. "To what do I owe this pleasure, Father?"

Richard flicked hair out of his face as he spoke in his usual unaffected tone. "I found a replacement for Chase."

The knot formed again, bigger this time, and Holden had trouble speaking around it. He also had a hard time ignoring the icicles forming along his spine and the dread in his gut. Holden hadn't seen his half brother since the night of Jericho's murder, except for his appearances in one of Holden's eerily vivid dreams—images of Chase strapped down on a metal slab, or strung up in a device constructed of tight straps, as a man with a thin black band tattooed around his bright-green eyes leaned over him.

"Chase isn't replaceable."

Richard mirrored Holden's pose and said nothing.

"Unless you've located another multitalented psy who was psychically *and* physically intimidating enough to safeguard the club? I'm a little skeptical about that possibility since Chase was practically superhuman."

Richard's jaw clenched, and something passed over his face that Holden had never seen before. Hurt? Frustration? Whatever it had been, it was gone in an instant. "Apparently not, since he allowed himself to be controlled and nearly killed by a void."

Holden narrowed his eyes. "Beck wasn't a void. She absorbed powers and took them as her own. She was as close to a psychic vampire as a real person can get, even though you and the other leaders have always said that was a myth."

"Regardless, your brother didn't sense her hidden ability despite being *nearly superhuman*."

"Neither did you," Holden said sharply. "And you put her here."

The silence that fell between them was sharp enough to slice holes in Holden's self-control. There was so much he wanted to say to his father about that situation. Pointing out that *no one* in the Community had identified Beck for what she was until Theo and Nate Black had come along was only one of them.

If it weren't for the Black twins, it was entirely possible Beck would have continued using Evolution as her honeypot to cannibalize powerful psychics. But Holden couldn't say those things because he'd sworn his silence to Nate, and he couldn't let his father know that, at the back of his mind, he put a big chunk of the blame on *him*. For not vetting better, for not trying harder to get past someone's mental shields before putting them in a position of authority, and for blaming Chase.

But making those accusations, and asking those questions, would cast him in the kind of light Theo had been in before his death. A shit stirrer, a blasphemer, someone who didn't trust the Community and who was likely a troublemaker. But the big difference was Theo hadn't been a member, and Holden had been born into all this.

So he smiled and nodded.

"Tell me about the new guy." Holden couldn't resist a dig. "Was your vetting process more thorough than it was with Beck, or did you leave out mistresses this time?"

Richard had no tells, so it was impossible to know whether he was close to leaving in disgust or backhanding Holden before going on a rant about what could happen if people found him disloyal, before sending him off to be realigned at the Farm. Either was possible, and both had happened before.

"His name is Six."

Holden wrinkled his nose. "'Six'?"

"It's short for Sixtus. Sixtus Rossi. I would think you'd remember him, considering how you behaved at his hearing."

Rolling the name around in his head summoned an image of a thin, olive-skinned teenager with fierce eyes so dark they'd looked black. It was a face Holden hadn't seen, or thought about, for years. He only remembered it because his encounter with Six had hung over his head like a pall for many years. Or more accurately, him witnessing how the Community had treated Six had hung over him.

It'd been the first time he'd feared the founders. And when he'd first learned that breaking Community rules could have serious consequences.

Over a decade ago, the biggest scandal to rock the Community had been a break-in at Community Watch—the organization run by the Comm that supported young and displaced psychics with no family of their own.

Six, a formerly homeless youth who'd been taken in by CW to be aligned and rehabilitated to become a Comm member, had raided and robbed the place. Holden had only known about it as a teenager because his father had taken him to the tribunal that had followed—where they'd discussed Six's consequences. Before that, Holden hadn't known tribunals existed for rule breakers. Or that they were public for anyone in the Comm to come and bear witness to a troublemaker receiving their sentence.

Even as the punk kid Holden had been at the time, it had shaken him. Somewhere, in the back of his mind, he'd known that there were real laws in the world. Real police and judicial systems. And the deepest part of his brain—the part *he'd* receive consequences for even having since it was the part full of doubts and dangerous questions—whispered that the tribunal seemed illegal. Thankfully, it had only been his father who had seemed to sense Holden's thoughts, and Richard had sent him warning stares between debates.

Besides Six's consequences—going to the Farm to be realigned for an unknown period of time—the founders had argued over whether it was worth it to take in people with no connections or "value" to the Community. Most members weren't like Holden, born into connections and money. Most were disenfranchised, had no family, or had been institutionalized for claiming to have psychic powers. These people were the most vulnerable, and required the most effort by the Community to realign and rehabilitate them, but they always turned out to be the most loyal.

Except for Six.

Six had been present at the board meeting, sitting in a chair removed from everyone, and they'd talked about him as if he couldn't hear them.

As loyal as Holden had always been to the Comm, it was the first time he'd realized how cutthroat they could be. How they played judge and jury with the lives of Community members regardless of their age. He'd vowed to never get on their bad sides. And he'd ached for the thin teenager with the burning dark eyes who'd sat staring at everyone fiercely. Defiantly.

That defiance had been almost intoxicating, because Holden had never seen anyone look at his father that way before. He'd wondered how anyone could be so brave, and had gazed at the mysterious, dark-eyed boy as Six was dragged out. They'd only made eye contact for a brief moment after Holden had whispered to his father and asked whether Six would be okay, and whether they could help.

So weird how that memory was still perfectly etched into Holden's mind.

"The kid who robbed CW?" Holden asked skeptically. "The reason why they started sending more 'challenging' intakes to the Farm before they advanced further?"

"Yes." Richard seemed pleased that Holden's memory was sound. "After the years he spent working at the Farm, he became an invaluable member of the Community."

"Color me skeptical and yet still intrigued."

"He's an invulnerable," Richard said. "He has a natural mental shield that prevents him from being susceptible to psychic abilities. Due to that, he's excellent at positions requiring security."

"I thought that was a myth," Holden said, frowning. "Then again I'd also thought psy vampires were a myth, so never mind."

Richard pursed his lips, staring flatly, and only went on after determining Holden was done speaking. "Invulnerables are not a myth. They're rare, but if found, they make excellent guards. We can't trust every psy who shows up on the CW's doorstep, and it's a huge security risk if we let the wrong one in and told them our secrets only to have them be turned against us. An invulnerable security force would safeguard the place against mental and physical attacks, and Six piloted that program. He'll be an asset to you and this nightclub since you insist on keeping it open."

Holden raised a skeptical eyebrow. He could see how having an impenetrable brain guarding the place would be great against a psychic attack, but . . . it just meant they had no idea what their invulnerable guards were thinking. Or whether they were really loyal.

"Why wouldn't I keep it open?" he asked. "Queer psychics need safe places too." Richard just looked at him flatly, and Holden rolled his eyes. "Aren't you worried he's untrustworthy?"

"No. That was nearly fifteen years ago, and he's moved past it. During his detention and realignment, we realized that due to Six being an invulnerable, it's difficult for him to empathize with others. He doesn't feel things the way the average person does, and he doesn't always make decisions based on an understanding of how other people will react."

"So he robbed the organization that took him off the street because he didn't consider how they'd feel about it? Huh. Sounds like a sociopath to me. Seems like your invulnerable-guard plan may have a flaw."

"He's not a sociopath," Richard said sharply, giving Holden pause. He'd never seen his father be defensive over another person before. Not even him or Chase. "He has a capacity to feel and understand other people, he just processes things differently because of his internal shield."

"Uh-huh."

A mental shield so strong it prevented Six from possessing even a normal human's basic level of empathy. Holden wondered how it worked. Was it possible to turn it off and on? Didn't sound like it. A talent like that frankly sounded like torture and a permanent roadblock to making lasting interpersonal relationships, although . . . apparently Richard had formed an attachment to Six.

"What was he doing before coming here to guard the gay club?" Holden asked. "I'm sure it's his dream job."

"He was head of security at the Farm."

The guy was going from being head of security at a major Community facility to . . . head of security at an LGBT nightclub. A wave of irritation washed over Holden's grim amusement.

"Tell me something, Father. Is your new guy a replacement for Chase, in terms of safeguarding the club, or is he also a replacement for Beck . . . which means he's monitoring me?"

The answer came in the form of pursed lips and the distant pump of bass as the DJ finally set up inside the club. The dubstep drops of a pop song's remix were annoying enough on their own, but somehow the soundtrack was embarrassing with his father standing there. Richard was probably wondering why he'd financed a queer club for psychics that had proved far more trouble than it was worth.

"I think you know the answer to that, Holden."

Holden's nostrils flared. "Why? Beck caused the disappearances, she killed Theo, and she killed Jericho. She tried to kill me *and* Chase."

"You failed to identify the threat, thereby putting others at risk."

"The threat that *you* put here." Holden jutted a finger at his father. "With all due respect, Father, I think you're either beginning to suffer from dementia, or you're in complete denial about what happened in this club. It was your puppet who harmed our community, and instead of apologizing for putting me and my people in harm's way, you ship my brother off to who the hell knows where, and you give me another babysitter—a fucking sociopath shield thing."

"Holden." Two syllables had never resembled a thunderclap as much as Holden's name when his father said it. "Your two biggest flaws are your lack of self-control and your mouth. Learn to control one and you may have less trouble with the other. Until then, I suggest you not presume you're entitled to an explanation. If you trusted the Community, you wouldn't be demanding one."

"I *do* trust the Community. But after what happ—"

"What *happened* didn't just happen to you," Richard said, finally showing the first bits of emotion. His steely-eyed facade cracked, and he moved closer to Holden. "It happened to the entire Community. Seeds of distrust have been sown because you weren't able to handle the situation with Beck discreetly. Police should not have been called to the scene of Jericho's death, and after Beck was taken down, you should have *only* called me and me alone. If you were anyone else, you'd be gone, Holden. Do you understand that?"

Holden did understand, but he could do nothing but stare. Repeating his father's accusations verbally would have had no effect, but they ran through his mind.

He was at fault for not helping to cover up the crimes? For not hiding that a high-ranking Community member had committed them. *He* had failed the Community by bringing in outsiders? Maybe they thought he was more at fault than Beck in that regard.

And if they truly believed that, who knew what they thought of Chase, whose purpose had been to identify, evaluate, and eliminate threats from Evolution. Was he at a tribunal somewhere like Six had been so long ago? Had board members determined what his fate would be for failing them, while he sat in a corner with no ability to participate in his fate? Did any of them matter as individuals or did they only matter if they remained dedicated members of the Community?

"I see," was all he managed.

Richard watched him for a moment before nodding. "Six will be starting immediately."

"How immediately?"

Richard indicated one of the monitors. Holden followed the direction of his father's finger and zeroed in on the camera in the VIP section. He caught only a glimpse of a tall man with ridiculously broad shoulders and huge biceps covered in tattoos before the figure was out of range.

"Now."

CHAPTER TWO

T he man who walked into the office did not remotely resemble the teen boy who'd just strolled through his memories. Adult Sixtus was slightly taller than Holden and corded with about thirty more pounds of muscle. His biceps were nearly bursting from his sleeves, and his pecs were clearly visible beneath the too-small black polo he wore, making the typically conservative style look like the prequel to a stripping routine in *Magic Mike*. He also wore khaki pants so tight his thighs looked like they were being strangled. He'd paired the two articles of clothing with scuffed motorcycle boots with steel toes.

Holden didn't make an attempt to hide his slow ogle, and dragged his eyes from boots to crotch to clavicle before taking in Six's face. His fathomless black eyes were the only familiar feature in that olive-skinned face. He had a full beard and mustache, thick black hair tied up in a bun, and wide lips that Holden wanted to suck on. Why did his sociopathic handler have to be a disgustingly sexy lumberjack hipster?

"Huh," Holden said. "He's filled out."

Richard went back to pursing his lips, but Sixtus didn't even blink. He didn't scan Holden or react to the intense eye-fuck he'd just received. There seemed to be nothing behind those dark eyes. The effect was more disturbing when Holden, by default, reached out with his gift to get an impression. He'd expected a hint of impatience or irritation even if it was muted by the mental shield that was apparently always in place, but he felt nothing.

Theo Black had had a powerful mental shield, and Holden had been able to bypass it more often than not. Not with Six, though.

All Holden received was a faint shock, as if he'd tried to touch Six's mind and had been hit with a burst of static electricity.

Invulnerable indeed. This was going to be unnerving.

Holden's irritation reared up again.

"Do you speak?" he asked. "Or are you just going to stand there and stare at me like a robot?"

Six looked at Richard. "Did you tell him?"

"I told him everything," Richard said. "He's not used to people not fawning all over him, so it may take him some getting used to."

Heat flooded Holden's face. His hands balled.

"Fine." Six moved past Holden, shoulders brushing, and surveyed the wall of cameras. "This is outdated. There shouldn't be more than one or two terminals that you can use to monitor every camera. Why didn't you install one?"

It took a minute for Holden to realize Six was talking to him.

"Excuse me?"

"Why haven't you updated your security system?"

"What— Wait. Excuse the hell out of me, but you don't even greet your new employer before going into a criticism of his setup?"

Six finally turned, one of his thick dark brows arched. "'Employer'? The Community is my employer. You own this nightclub, and that's fine, but I don't work for you."

Holden looked from Six to his father, trying to figure out why he was surprised by this turn of events when it was exactly what he'd just deduced moments ago. Six wasn't stepping into Chase's shoes—he was taking over for both Chase and Beck.

"If you have a problem with my security system, I suggest you write up your critique and your suggestions for me to peruse at a later time. I'm not having this conversation here, now, or in front of him," Holden said, flicking his fingers at his father. "And if you're here as security, I'd also suggest you get down to the floor and observe my failure of a bouncer. Maybe you can step in for him since you're an expert. Model what it means to be a good doorman and hope he can copy your technique."

Six stared at him for a long moment, gaze not flickering and expression not shifting from the blank mask, before he inclined his head. "Fine. I'll shadow him until he seems less like an incompetent piece of shit."

Holden's jaw dropped as Six once again brushed past him and strode out the door. He stared through the darkened doorway for several seconds before pointing at his father.

"You've lost your mind."

"It will be fine, Holden."

"No. No, it won't. He is insolent—"

"Insolent?" Richard barked out a laugh. "I just told you he doesn't perceive emotions the way we do. He never learned to temper his speech and body language to make other people comfortable. He's better than he used to be."

"Well, that's very special." Holden couldn't keep the sarcasm out of his voice. "I love a good heartwarming story about the wayward psy babies you've taken in. But unfortunately for you, this one isn't going to work out. I won't have some jackass from the Bronx talking down to me in my own club. Especially in front of my other employees. It creates a confusing chain of command and—"

"Holden," his father snapped. "It's a nightclub, not the government of a small country. If you can't handle this, it's no wonder you couldn't handle the situation with Beck."

Holden's mouth shut with an audible click.

Richard's eyes narrowed. "If your concern is that you won't be able to control or seduce him, you *should* be worried. It won't work. It's part of the reason I chose him." Richard turned his back on Holden and walked to the door. "I was wrong about what I said before. Your biggest weaknesses are your mouth, your lack of self-control, and your dick. You need one employee who won't fall for your bullshit, and then maybe you can rise to your full potential and be the leader I know you can be."

A thousand disrespectful responses flew to mind, but Holden knew when he could push, and every retort crossed a number of boundaries. Boundaries that would take him beyond the point of being Richard Payne's sassy gay son to being . . . something else. The type of Community member who showed insubordination to upper-tier members, and who would benefit from a trip to the Farm for "realignment." It'd happened to Holden a lot in his younger years, but for Richard Payne's son to go there as an adult would be an embarrassment for them both. An unforgivable one.

The club filled quickly on Friday nights, and this one was no exception. They were packed by eleven o'clock with a healthy line snaking down the length of the building and toward Ninth Avenue. Once they reached capacity, it was time for the doorman to start cherry-picking people from the line. They went by regular customers and members of the Comm.

Stefen had always been a complete failure at this aspect of the job. He hated telling people no, even if it meant hearing a rant from Holden when the Comm folk wound up filling message boards with negative reviews because it took so long to get in. To Holden's royal annoyance, Six was excellent at the job. He handpicked Evo regulars as if he could sense they belonged to the Community. It was impossible, but his precision was uncanny. Through the outdated monitor system, Holden had spent a couple of hours watching his new handler in action. He stood straight, shoulders thrown back and intimidating even in his preppy polo and khaki pants, and he looked at everyone in line as if they meant nothing to him. As if they *were* nothing until they got into the club.

Truth be told, it wasn't that serious. Evolution had an air of exclusivity because they prioritized Comm members, but it'd gained traction with voids as well. The harder it was to get in, the more people showed up, and the more its reputation of being an extremely elite queer club spread. Stefen had briefly put a dent in the rumors of impenetrability, but it seemed like Six would be fixing that in no time. Likely because he, too, was impenetrable.

And what would it *be* like to penetrate someone like Six? A stoic man with a mental shield that prevented him from experiencing the world like everyone else. Had he ever walked into a funeral service and wept due to the stench of grief in the room? Laid a comforting hand on the shoulder of a friend in need? Understood that *I'm fine* usually meant the speaker was anything but? Had he ever felt the heat of someone else's lust, or did he need a direct *I want to fuck you* to get a clue? Most people didn't experience those things on the same level as an empath like Holden, but Six apparently even lacked the ability to pick up on cues that voids *could* feel.

Holden forced himself to stop staring at Six and leave his office.

The bass from the music assaulted him as soon as he was in the hallway. A throb started in his temple and spread. He brought down his mental shield firmly, not wanting to absorb any extra vibes and make the pain worse.

Holden respected Richard Payne for founding the Community, but interacting with him was nerve-racking. Holden usually spent the entire conversation waiting to be told what was wrong with him or how he'd most recently failed or let the Community down, while his stomach twisted and churned. The thing was, their relationship wasn't out of the ordinary for the Community. As a whole, it valued ties to the organization more than biological family.

Holden's mother had been different. If it wasn't for Jessica Payne, he wouldn't have known relationships with one's parents could be anything other than tense and distant. Unfortunately, she'd long since gone to live on the Farm away from Richard, and Holden rarely saw her.

The VIP section was mostly void of customers, except for a couple already kissing in one of the alcoves. Holden made it to the spiral staircase leading to the lower floor without incident, but someone grabbed his upper arm as soon as he descended.

Even so many months after the night of Jericho's murder, Holden's heart caught in his throat. He froze, eyes widening and pulse racing, and was overcome with an instinct to yank away and run. But he didn't. He took a deep breath, stared straight ahead, and reminded himself that Beck was gone, and Nate and Trent were in hiding. The night of the attack would never be repeated. There was no longer any danger here.

Evolution was safe.

"Holden?"

Holden cleared his throat, blinked away the lingering fear, and turned to face Elijah. Pasting on a smile, he tried to project calmness and authority. Waste of effort. Elijah had clearly been through better times and was unlikely to be worrying about Holden's state of mind.

The Dreadnought drummer had always been petite, but he was now perilously thin. His brown skin was pale and circles lined his eyes. Instead of his usual ensemble of short shorts, boots or Chuck Taylors, and a cut-up T-shirt, he was swimming in a hooded sweatshirt and loose jeans.

"Elijah. I haven't seen you in months."

Elijah ran a hand through his hair, gaze sweeping left and right before focusing on Holden again. In the past, he'd have leaped into Holden's arms or pulled him into a grope-y hug, but now he fidgeted with his sleeves and shifted from foot to foot. "Do you think we can go somewhere to talk?"

"I've been holed up in my office for too long as it is. Can it wait until I do my rounds?"

Elijah bit his lower lip.

"You're welcome to do them with me."

"Okay."

The relief in Elijah's face was concerning. Had he thought Holden would turn him away after all that had happened?

Frowning, Holden pulled the slighter man into a brief hug before leading him on a stroll of the club's perimeter. The dance floor was already packed, the lounges full of people sharing bottles and laughing, and the new bartenders were handling the influx of customers with ease. The best thing in the world Holden had done was to invest in bartenders who'd actually studied mixology, instead of people who'd just worked behind a bar in college. Wait times were shorter and the tendency for bartenders to over-pour was nearly eliminated.

"The place looks different," Elijah said quietly. "Did you tear down the stage?"

"Yes. After what happened . . ." Holden glanced at the space where the stage had once been. He'd had it removed and expanded the dance floor. "I guess I couldn't bear having other bands come in. It was a constant memory of what had happened, and it frankly felt disrespectful."

"I wouldn't have felt that way. Neither would Taína or Lia."

"I know, but after losing two out of five members of the band . . . it was just . . ." The confidence he'd been trying to project was steadily dissipating. "It was too hard."

They paused at the edge of the dance floor, and Holden made a conscious effort to take the measure of the crowd who'd shown up tonight. There were very few unfamiliar faces. Six was somehow doing an amazing job of prioritizing Comm members. As Holden eyeballed a couple whose dancing was starting to border on public sex rather than raunchy grinding, Elijah snagged his hand.

"Thanks for not being weird to me."

"Why would I be weird to you?"

"Because I went AWOL. The guy at the door almost refused to let me in. I had to name-drop you."

Holden stopped grilling the couple to stare at Elijah. "Pardon?"

"He like . . . interrogated me about where I've been. I dunno. It was weird as fuck."

A bolt of anger lit through Holden. He tightened his hand around Elijah's, abandoned his rounds, and walked quickly in the direction of the patio. With the music only a soft hum on the other side of the door, and the gate lined with small white Christmas lights, it was almost cozy. A good escape from the bustle of the club, and one of the few places besides his office that he could go to think when he was overwhelmed by memories, or the evening, or life in general. Which happened far too much lately.

"The doorman is new. Started tonight and instated by my father." Holden said that part through gritted teeth, swallowing bitterness at having to admit it to someone who'd once looked up to him. "He's worked security for the Comm for years. I don't know why he'd be grilling you about your whereabouts."

Elijah curled up in one of the metal chairs, pulling his knees up beneath his chin. "If he's a Community puppet, I get it. They've been trying to drag me to CW for counseling, but I'm really . . . not about that right now."

"Understandable. Nothing remains confidential." Holden sat on the edge of the chair opposite Elijah but leaned forward so he could keep his voice low. "Why've they been trying to pull you in?"

"I don't know. But they've basically been stalking me. I was staying with Taína in Brooklyn, but Comm spooks kept knocking on the door and trying to give me an escort to the CW. She was getting freaked out, and I was too, after one of them mentioned realignment, which basically means going to the Farm to be talked at forever about why the Community is this amazing godsend for a poor bummy psy like me . . . blah."

Holden slowly nodded and ran his eyes over Elijah. He was different. Everything from the way he held himself to his tone of voice was a far cry from the enthusiastic boy who'd volunteered at the CW and given testimonials about how the Community had saved him.

"I don't remember you being this cynical," Holden said.

"I didn't use to be this cynical. I used to think the Comm was a godsend that would keep me and my people safe." Elijah laughed dryly. "What a joke that turned out to be. They sent a predator to infiltrate an LGBT space because they didn't care enough to vet her and make sure she wasn't a threat. All they cared about was *someone* making sure Evolution wasn't making too many waves. When it comes down to it, everyone is just out for themselves."

"You mean my father is."

Elijah met his eyes. "Yes. Sorry, but yes. If he cared more, he wouldn't have sent a murderer. There's no way *no one* knew she was twisted by resentment and hate. Maybe they knew, and they dropped her here to get rid of her? It's not like we matter to them."

"I see what you're saying but . . ." But what? It was likely true. And yet Holden couldn't help but defend his father. The Community. The people who'd allowed him to have this privileged life instead of growing up misunderstood and paranoid about his abilities like so many other young psys. "I just hope they learn from this experience even though it's too late to make amends."

"They can't make amends, and they don't even try." Elijah dropped his feet with a thump. "Anyway, that's not why I wanted to talk to you. I want to know where Chase is."

"I don't know, Elijah."

"But you're his brother."

"Yes, but that doesn't mean anyone tells me anything. As you said, my last name may be Payne, but my primary function is still just the owner of an LGBT space within the Community. I'm not privy to confidential—"

"Why is it confidential?" Elijah demanded. "Chase didn't do anything wrong. If anything, he tried to get me out before any of that went down—"

"What?" Holden's eyes narrowed. "When?"

Elijah's gaze dropped. He pressed his hands together. "He'd been trying to convince me to get out of town since Theo died. Was killed."

"How . . ." Holden pressed his fingers to his head, briefly closing his eyes. "Let me get this straight. My brother *knew* there was a danger in the club, a danger that put you at risk, and he didn't say anything . . . to me?"

"He didn't even explain himself to me," Elijah said quickly. "He just kept stressing that he wanted me to leave before things got bad. When I asked him to explain, he . . . I don't even know, Holden. It was so strange. It was like he literally couldn't explain it to me. He'd start to say something, and he'd stammer and break into a sweat, before finally snarling at me to just trust him. Every single time."

Holden's eyes narrowed. "I don't understand."

"I didn't understand either, but there was definitely something he wanted to tell me and couldn't. I'm betting it's the same reason he didn't tell you. And why . . . he instead found a way to get Nate here so he could pick up where Theo left off."

The explanation was at once overly convoluted and the most straightforward theory that had come up so far. He'd wondered why Nate had shown up in New York, how he'd found out the things he had, and why Chase would have sent *him* visions instead of a brother in the same city. One he worked with and saw every day. But he'd never gotten answers to those questions, because Chase had never come back.

"Maybe Beck was exerting her control over him and preventing him from speaking?"

Elijah shook his head. "She would have killed him. There's no way she knew that he knew about her. That's why he kept putting on his asshole act so hard when Nate got here—to keep up the appearance that he was all on board with her. I just don't know what was holding him back. And I don't know how he knew what was coming when no other precogs saw it."

Holden ran a hand through his hair. Only then did he realize it was trembling. "Talking about this makes me feel sick."

"Same, but . . . I can't stop. We need to find Chase. I just have this awful feeling that he's in trouble." Elijah rubbed his hands together before dragging them along the knees of his jeans. "I keep having these dreams . . . that he's like . . . strapped down. And there's this scary guy—"

Holden's heart leaped. Images from his own dreams rushed back, and he clearly saw the man with the cat eyes.

"Does he have a tattooed band around—"

For the second time that evening, a door opened abruptly and interrupted Holden. This time, instead of Richard Payne, it was his puppet. Six.

Elijah automatically curled in on himself again, glaring up at Six from beneath his wild brown curls. Six stared back impassively before turning his attention to Holden.

"Stefen is following my lead. I'm going to assess your security and begin making preparations for upgrades."

"No, you're not. My security has been fine."

"Given the disappearances you were unable to track with your surveillance system and the murder, I would say it's a fucking failure." The words were harsh, but there was no heat in them. Six didn't even raise his voice. He said it matter-of-fact, as though it were a normal way to converse with other people. After a beat, he looked at Elijah. "You should be encouraging Comm members to check in at the CW. It's what Richard expects."

Elijah flipped him off without comment. Six didn't react.

Holden frowned, looking between the two. "That expectation has never been made clear to me. I didn't realize we were supposed to check in, and I was raised in the Comm."

"Well, you've never been part of an investigation. Now you are." Six jerked his chin at Elijah. "So is he. Get him to the CW, or I'll make a call."

Elijah tensed. Holden crossed his arms over his chest.

"Elijah, why don't you let me and Six have a moment? I'll find you in a bit."

"Sounds great."

Elijah shot Six one last glower before hurrying inside, likely out of the club and to the subway. Holden had forgotten to ask where he was staying now.

The door shut with a bang, but Six didn't jump. He didn't do anything. Just stood there in his skintight polo and khakis, looking both absolutely gorgeous and like a blank slate. His lack of expression was alarming.

"Do you understand that you're being a fucking asshole?" Holden asked.

Six raised an eyebrow. "No? I'm just telling you facts. Richard expects Comm members to check in on the regular, especially members who are involved in an active investigation."

"'An active investigation,'" Holden repeated. "Meaning the investigation surrounding Beck."

"Surrounding all of you."

"Excuse me?"

"The board is looking into all of you. They want to know how the perpetrator was allowed to prey on Comm members in this club for months, and how the psys who run the place never noticed. You'll probably get off easy because of your last name," he said bluntly. "But the others? Maybe not."

Holden's eyes widened, and he took a step forward. "What the fuck are you talking about? They're the ones who put her here! If my father, or the board, are investigating anyone, it should be themselves." For the first time, a flicker of something crossed Six's countenance. Interest? Intrigue? Holden had no idea, and he was too fired up to try to figure it out. "I have no idea why they're trying to redirect the blame and find a scapegoat, but I won't have you harassing my employees, my customers, or my friends. The next time you have a question, you ask *me*. Or I will kick your ass out of here regardless of what my father or the *board* has to say about it."

"That won't happen, but duly noted."

Holden wanted to punch him. Punch him until he bled all over his goddamn beard. He didn't know what was more infuriating—the dismissal or the calm tone it was said in. Richard had said Six didn't perceive emotion the way others did, but did he even feel them?

Again, Holden reached out with his gift, but this time it was like a steel gate slamming shut on him. The connection was cut off violently.

"Don't try to read me," Six said. "It won't work. And I can feel it. If you don't want me fucking with your friends, you stay out of my head."

"Oh? Does it bother you, Sixtus?"

"Yes. I frankly find you people creepy, and I'm glad I can keep you out." Again with the brutal honesty in that flat tone. "Your father warned me you try to influence people with your gift, but rest assured—it won't work with me. Don't bother. You can't affect my mood or my opinion, and you can't seduce me with your little brain tricks."

Holden forced a smirk that likely resembled a snarl. "So I can seduce you in other ways?"

"You'll never find out if you keep relying on your empath shit, instead of the words and actions the rest of our species have utilized since we first evolved." Six looked Holden over once, twice, then scoffed. "Put it to you like this: stay out of my head or I'll beat the shit out of you."

"First you challenge me to seduce you and now you threaten me. Does my father know you're this kinky?"

"Your father doesn't know a lot about me." Six turned to the door. "I'm going to fix your shitty security system. Don't bother arguing. Your opinion is literally worthless."

He was gone before Holden could get in a last word.

CHAPTER THREE

Holden's opinion did turn out to be worthless.

In the week following Six's abrupt intrusion into his life, they'd bickered over the security system until Holden had demanded they put it to a vote with the rest of Evolution's crew. Surprisingly, Six had agreed. Unfortunately, the entire crew had voted against Holden.

"You're a traitor."

Kamryn, one of the new bartenders, didn't look up from wiping down the bar. She cleaned it constantly throughout the day. Given Holden's tendency to binge watch old episodes of *Bar Rescue*, he didn't poke fun at her for it.

"You're being silly," she said. "It's a good idea. The old system was ancient."

"It worked perfectly fine."

"Holden, you're being difficult because you don't like him."

"I have no strong feelings about his existence one way or the other." Holden examined his reflection in the mirror behind the bar. He tucked hair behind his ear and tried not to pay attention to Six moving through the room behind him. It was a Wednesday night, so the place wasn't as packed as it normally was. Now that they didn't have live music, they attracted even less of a crowd at off-peak times, so he had no problem tracking Six as he went from the staircase to the patio. For such a big person, he was light-footed and moved with a certain elegance that was eye-catching.

"Did you just zone out while staring at your own reflection?"

Holden's gaze snapped back to Kamryn. "No. I was watching our head of security. He's always prowling around."

Kamryn rolled her eyes. "He's really not that bad. It's not that serious, Holden."

"'Not that bad,'" he repeated. "How?"

"He's a little strange because he's so straight-faced all the time, but he's polite. Sometimes it seems as though he is actually trying to be friendly but doesn't know how. It's endearing."

Holden looked between her and Six's reflection. "I'm sorry, are we talking about the same cyborg?"

She snorted. "Yes. He even told some of us that his primary concern with having the security revamped is so nothing like what happened in the past can happen again."

Now *that* put Holden's back up. He drew to his full height and crossed his arms over his chest. "I'm not sure what he means by that."

"Oh, come on, Holden. The disappearances? The murders? We all know, we still chose to work here anyway because we trust you and the Community to keep us out of harm's way this time around. The way I see it, that's what Six is trying to do as well. He doesn't have the social skills to be . . . charismatic about it."

"I'm so glad you've gotten to know him that well. Did you also discuss the childhood trauma that turned him into a complete ass?"

Kamryn held up a wineglass, inspecting it to ensure not a single particle clung to it. One of her big brown eyes focused on Holden through it as she arched an eyebrow. "We didn't have personal conversations, boss. Just him trying to make me feel less awkward while he was installing cameras in my domain." She put the glass down and swept an arm out around the bar. "If you stopped snarling and pissing all over the club to mark it as your own, you'd probably get along better and be less stressed out."

"Oh, is that so?"

"Mm-hmm. You could try getting laid too."

Holden scoffed. "Trust me, that's not an issue."

"So then talk to your security dude and stop being so damn extra."

Heaving a loud sigh, Holden eased off the bar chair. "Fine. I'll go ask him to finally show me how the new computers work. But first— have you seen Elijah today?"

She shook her head. "Not since last night. He was looking for you but was acting pretty cagey."

"Hmm. Okay, thanks."

"No problem."

Holden turned away from the bar, bypassing a small cluster of baby psys who were approaching for a drink. There had been a time when he'd been unable to spot a psychic in a crowd of voids, and he'd thought that was the way it was supposed to be. After all, he wasn't a spotter like Beck. He couldn't sense them. But . . . if he deliberately reached out with his gift, he could pick up on vibes that were just a little different from the average person. Everybody had emotions, but psys had this extra crackle of electricity that served almost as a signal to Holden that, *Yes, this was someone like him.* Someone different. Someone who also belonged to this group of misfits with gifts who'd come together as a family.

Holden was now wondering whether the family aspect of the Community was shifting away. As a kid, it had all seemed so magical—the outreach they'd done to find young or disconnected psychics, and the feeling of belonging that Holden had picked up from everyone during the holiday parties and gatherings, group vacations, campouts, community-building trips . . . But over time things had changed. Or, maybe, after the last few months, he'd begun to change into someone more cynical. Someone warier. And the more his father pushed back on any questions about their actions, the more his wariness heightened.

Holden reached the stairs just as Six returned to them. They stopped at the same time, facing each other with some awkwardness before Six headed to the upper level without a word. Sighing again, Holden followed. Once they were in the cramped office, Holden said, "I thought you could show me how to use my new security system. Do you have time?"

"Yes. I was just adjusting the cameras outside."

Six was sitting behind the desk, once again clad in a skintight polo buttoned up all the way but this time paired with cargo pants. As he sat on the edge of the chair with his thighs spread, Holden was waiting for all those muscles to burst the seams.

"Why do you dress like an extra from *Jersey Shore*?"

"I'd have to pop my collar for that." He only paused in his typing when a surprised laugh fell from Holden's mouth. Raising an eyebrow, Six said, "Was I not supposed to get the reference?"

"Well, you're a cyborg, so I didn't think you would."

Six turned in the chair so he was facing Holden. He had on his default neutral face, but a slight twitch of his brow and lip betrayed possible amusement at the comment. Was there some getting through to him after all, or were they destined to stare at each other in mutual blankness to see who could emote the least for the next . . . however long he'd be here as Holden's handler?

"Not having an empathy chip doesn't make me a cyborg. There are plenty of ways to figure someone out without feeling any of their vibes."

Holden crossed his arms over his chest and leaned against the wall next to the desk. "As someone who was born with an empathy chip with elephantiasis, color me skeptical."

Six mirrored his post, crossing his arms and leaning back in the chair with his thighs spread. The view of thick thighs and a good-sized bulge was a temptation Holden didn't try to resist. He glanced down twice before managing to hold Six's steady gaze.

"You rely too much on your psychic shit," Six said. "Not having those abilities makes me more observant."

"I'm extremely observant."

"Yeah? Then how did you have a full-on Investigation Discovery series going on right under your nose?"

Holden pursed his lips. "I was supposed to guess there was such a thing as a psychic vampire in real life?"

"Maybe not, but you could be better at reading people's body language and demeanor when they're good at shielding their thoughts and emotions." Six pointed at Holden with his two fingers pressed together like a gun. "That's rule number one—never trust another psychic's vibes. There's a good chance someone up to no good has managed to mask their vibes or project something different from what they're actually feeling."

"Whose rules are these?"

"Mine."

"Huh. I'll play along. What's rule number two?"

"Don't let your other senses weaken because all you do is rely on the sixth one. You have two eyes, a nose, ears, hands, and a mouth. Don't forget to use them."

Holden grinned. "Don't worry, handsome. I never forget how to use my mouth."

"That remains to be seen. I heard it was Stefen on his knees."

It was the best comeback Holden had been hit with in a while, and he couldn't help snorting out a laugh. "Fuck, so you do have some kind of sense of humor."

Six shrugged. "Some kind. But don't get distracted. I'm serious. If all you do is rely on your talent, the senses everyone else is born with get weak. And what will happen when one day you're unable to use your empath chip?"

"That would never happen." At Six's flat look, Holden immediately doubted the claim. He just couldn't see *how* it would happen. "Fine. Why don't we test my powers of observation right now. I read you and you read me, and we can see whose reading is more accurate. Except . . ." Holden held up a finger. "You have to be honest."

"I don't lie."

"Everybody lies."

"The only people who say things like 'everybody lies' or 'everybody cheats' are shitty people who want to believe they aren't shitty."

"Heh. You may be onto something there." Holden pressed his shoulder blades against the wall, jutting out his hips and torso. Six didn't move despite the decreased proximity, but his eyes didn't stray either. "Okay. You go first."

Six stood to full height, a couple of inches taller. Holden tensed as if expecting to be twisted and turned for a full examination, but Six just keenly stared while tugging at his beard.

"You come from money, and while you love the things that gets you—like your tailored suits, expensive cologne, and high-dollar shaving equipment—you hate that everyone in the Community knows it. You hate that they know your father invested in this club and that he owns more of a share than you do."

Holden's back went straight, his hands closing into tight fists. Six sat on the edge of the desk.

"You've never had a real job before, and you've never had a real boss, so you don't know how to be one. You're like a kid in a candy store with all of these people to order around but also socialize with, and deep down you worry they actually can't stand you. They just do what you say because you're the boss and your last name is Payne."

Why had Holden thought this would be fun? Humiliation was the quickest entry point to rage, and he could feel anger soaring through his body to heat the collar of his four-figure, tailored shirt. Dampening his lips and widening his stance, he asked, "Anything else? Or was the purpose of your analysis just to tell me my staff doesn't like me?"

For the first time, Six's mouth stretched into a smile. Not a smirk, not a teeth-baring grin, just the subtlest shift of his lips that made him look softer and more approachable. "This isn't about them. I have no fucking clue what they think of you. I'm talking about your fears, Mr. Payne."

Some of the tension eased from Holden's body. "I see. Are you done?"

"Almost. You worry about all those things because you know deep down people are intimidated by your father. You know that because *you're* intimidated by your father. Your entire life is a double-edged sword of benefiting from his money and power while knowing it makes you look like a spoiled shit, and trying to do things on your own but being unable to assert yourself because he does things like issue you a fucking handler." Six jerked a thumb at himself. "So you make yourself feel better by enjoying the money and trying to fuck people who aren't initially interested in you because it makes you feel wanted and powerful when they finally give in, and it's all you have."

How do you know this?

The question was poised on the tip of Holden's tongue, but he bit back on it. Asking Six his methods, or accusing him of having some secret ability, would do nothing more than verify the—unfortunately accurate—claims he'd just made.

Holden had never felt so small in his life, and he'd never been so unsure of what to do with himself or how to respond. He stood still and held Six's gaze and wondered how they would manage to get through the next however many months with Holden knowing this man had picked him apart with barely any effort at all.

He cleared his throat. "My turn. But I need you standing."

Six stood again. "You didn't say if I was right."

Holden leveled him with a hard stare. "Do I need to confirm it for extra mortification?"

Six started to speak, paused, and shrugged. "Guess not."

"Exactly. Now let me conduct my own observations."

For the next few seconds, Holden made a big show of studying his subject. Six didn't flinch when Holden ran his fingers along his shirt sleeve, pulled at the back of his collar, or leaned in close enough to smell his scent—cheap soap and no aftershave, which made sense since he had the lumberjack thing going for him. He also didn't react when Holden touched his hands or when he walked his own fingers down the front of Six's shirt. There was no scientific reason for that other than wondering whether the man's chest and stomach were as hard as they appeared, or if he was sucking it in. The answer made Holden want to go back to the gym.

"Finished," he said, smiling. "You ready for my analysis?"

"Astound me," Six said flatly.

"I'll try my best." Holden resumed his lean against the wall. "You weren't prepared to take this position. In fact, I think it was thrust on you at the last minute, which is why all your business-casual attire was quickly swiped from a rack at a discount store judging by the thin scratchy material and lack of a tag in the back. You usually wear jeans and T-shirts—which is why your non-denim pants look a couple of sizes too small. Maybe you stopped wearing them after you started going so hard at CrossFit."

For the second time, Six flashed that cute smile. There was a dimple in his left cheek. Holden was determined to make it disappear forever by being as brutally honest as possible.

"But despite your muscular thighs and edible ass, you're not used to intimacy. You've not been with very many people sexually. There's a chance you might even be a virgin. That's why you don't react to intimate touches like me stroking your hands or the front of your chest. You assume I'm joking about my attraction because you can't feel my vibes, and you're not used to people touching you and it going anywhere sexually, so it doesn't make you nervous. You, sir, are an island." Six's mouth flattened into a line, and Holden smiled broadly. "How did I do?"

"Impressively."

"But how accurate was I?"

"Accurate enough for me to be impressed." Six turned away, once again sitting in the chair and facing the computer. "And more of a reason for you to not solely depend on your ability. You're much smarter than you look."

"Oh, why, thank you. You're so kind to me."

"You haven't given me reason to be kind."

"What if I tell you that business casual is unnecessary, and you don't have to wear those scratchy polos anymore?"

Six glanced down at his clothes. "Seriously?"

"Yes. You're security." Holden plucked at Six's collar and rubbed the material between his fingers again. "Besides, you're not my employee. You can do whatever you want."

"You have a point." Six stood and the inches between them diminished. "I can."

There was a fragment of a moment where their eyes met, and Holden wondered if there was something more behind that carefully even expression. A spark in those fathomless eyes. Intrigue, a challenge, or maybe even attraction? Whatever it was vanished before Holden could try to do another read, and then Six was jerking his chin at the computer.

"Let me show you how it works."

Releasing a slow breath, Holden took the seat Six had just occupied. His old desktop computer had been replaced by an enormous Apple product that was sleeker and fancier than any piece of technology Holden had ever owned. For all that he enjoyed spending his money, as Six had rightly declared, he didn't use it for things like phones or televisions or devices. Growing up, he'd never developed his peers' fascination with the new and shiny. He'd been preoccupied with the developing ability in his own mind.

"Are you gonna touch the mouse or just stare at your reflection in the monitor?"

"Oh, sorry."

Six snorted and began pointing to different icons until Holden navigated to the program that opened the interface that controlled the cameras. With two clicks, the entire array of monitors that had been in the cabinet were on the wide computer screen.

"You can rewind it too," Six said, hunched forward with his hand braced against the desk and his mouth an inch from Holden's ear. "Keep going. A little further back . . . There." Six leaned closer until his index finger nearly touched the screen. "What do you see?"

Holden realigned his synapses to stop reacting to his proximity to a man he should have disliked so he could focus on the minimized monitor Six had indicated. After making it bigger, Holden clearly saw Elijah heading out of the club with his hood up beneath a bomber jacket and his hands shoved in his pockets. He looked younger than usual with his hair sticking out of the hood and his shoulders hunched forward, as if he was trying to make himself appear small and invisible. Unfortunately for Elijah, he would always stand out due to his wild curls and striking features.

"How did you know I was looking for—"

"Don't just focus on the person you were looking for. There's more to see."

Holden's mouth shut as he frowned at the image again. There were the beginnings of a crowd swarming just behind Elijah, but as he scanned the faces and slowed down the speed of the video, he saw a couple of things. Two men turned in unison as soon as Elijah passed them, and after half a beat, they followed him out.

After replaying the moment a second time, Holden looked at Six. "Do you have others working with you? Following him?"

"No. I don't work with anyone."

"Then what the fuck was that about? Who *were* those guys?"

"I already told you." Six stood up straight. "They're watching all of you."

CHAPTER FOUR

It was December twenty-third and exactly six months since the last time Holden had spoken to his mother.

Intellectually, he knew that was odd. He knew other people didn't go long spans of time without speaking to their parents, especially their mothers, but it only struck a dull chord inside of him. Ever since Jessica Payne had relocated to the Farm about ten years ago, their communication had been minimal. The explanation had always been that she needed to get away from the city and her personality was better suited to the work on the Farm, but he'd always assumed that meant she needed to get away from his father. Understandable, but he'd been bitter that his only loving parent had become nonexistent in his life. Someone who only called on birthdays and holidays to vacantly inquire about his health before disappearing into yet another void where phones or computers apparently did not exist.

Holden usually tried to wait her out. See how long it would be before she picked up a phone and showed interest in her only child—since she refused to recognize Chase as even a stepson. Like clockwork, she typically called on Christmas. It was only two days away, but with strange men following Elijah and lingering in his club, Holden's game of telephone chicken would have to be put on the back burner.

He needed information, and he wasn't going to get it from his father.

As the drunken holiday party roared outside the office door, Holden inhaled his pride and made the call.

"The Verizon subscriber you're trying to reach is unavailable at this time."

Holden's hand tightened around the phone. He tapped his finger against her name again.

"The Verizon subscriber you're trying to reach is unavailable at this time."

Staring at his phone gave exactly zero insight, so he glared at the screen of surveillance footage instead. The VIP area was teeming with people and the lower level was even worse. The holiday party had always been a big attraction, but he'd worried this year would be slower due to the recent controversy. The inclusion of a Santa's Workshop-themed costume party had killed that concern. Every queer on this side of the East River had stormed Evolution in their most absurd elf costumes. It was so crowded that the psy population was diluted dramatically. Six was probably pissed.

Holden zeroed in on the front door, but saw Six had left Stefen to his own devices. A quick scan of the monitors showed that Six was standing in front of the patio door with his arms crossed and an expression of irritation on his face. He looked like the fucking Grim Reaper amid the green-and-red-sparkling people drunkenly dancing nearby. He'd taken Holden's advice to stop dressing like a frat boy and was outfitted in faded jeans with the knees ripped out, his usual steel-toed boots, and a T-shirt with the Harley-Davidson logo on the front. If not for the radio at his belt, he wouldn't have even looked like part of the staff. Which was good, because he wasn't. Although . . . he could make himself useful at the moment.

Holden jumped to his feet and strode out of the office, bypassing the crowd and evading the grasping hands of psys who recognized him and wanted his attention. Normally, he would have stopped to see if those hands belonged to someone fuckable, but he was on a mission.

Six's back was to him as he walked quickly down the corridor, but he turned to face Holden as if he'd sensed his presence. Which made absolutely no sense since he should have sensed . . . nothing. Holden filed that away for later.

"Can you—" His voice was lost in the music. "Can you do me a favor?" he repeated, louder.

Six still frowned. "What?"

Holden clenched his teeth and dropped a hand on one of Six's powerful shoulders before dragging him closer. Six tensed. He didn't resist, but he also held himself very still as Holden hissed in his ear.

"I know you used to work at the Farm, and I'm trying to get in touch with my mother."

"Why would I care?"

It was a struggle not to beat Six's head against the wall. "Is there a central number or something?"

"Probably."

Holden released a sound that was very close to a guttural growl. "Can you stop being a dickhead for once, and just tell me how to call? Please."

There was a beat of silence filled in by a remixed version of a classic Christmas song complete with electronic beats and YouTube sound bites. It was utterly ridiculous, and the longer it went on without either of them progressing this conversation, Holden was convinced he was wasting his time. But then Six's unreadable mien cracked as he lifted his muscular shoulders in a shrug.

"I'll text it to you. There's a main line, but it doesn't guarantee you'll get in contact with anyone."

"That literally makes no sense. Why would there be a main line if it doesn't lead to anyone?"

"Someone picks up, but that doesn't mean they'll help you. That's not how the Farm works."

"So how does it work?" When Six just stared at him with those fathomless black eyes, Holden waved an impatient hand. "Just give me the number."

He watched Six text him the number, nodded in thanks, and stepped out onto the marginally quieter patio. Someone had decorated it with Christmas lights and mistletoe. The absurd song was still penetrating the door and there was enough noise on the street to provide a real distraction, but he tried to shut it out as he waited for someone to pick up. Given it was a Friday evening, it wasn't the ideal time. But he'd always thought the place operated 24/7. Or at least that had always been his impression as a child.

"Good evening."

Holden started, having given up on someone answering. "Oh, hello. I know it's late, but I was hoping you could tell me how to contact a Community member who resides on the property."

"Is it a new admit? If so—"

"No, no. She's not a new psy. It's— I'm Holden Payne. I was hoping to get in touch with my mother." Silence greeted the declaration, and he cleared his throat. "My mother, Jessica Payne, has resided at the Farm for the past decade. My understanding is she was helping with the day-to-day operations management." The silence persisted. "I'm sorry, who am I speaking to?"

"Please hold, Mr. Payne."

"Wha—"

There was a click before he could finish his sentence. The line went silent for so long that he feared he'd been hung up on, but the phone still showed him as being connected. Even so, the wait dragged until he wound up sitting in one of the uncomfortable wicker chairs as two more horrific holiday songs played in their entirety. By the time the line clicked again, Holden had nearly given up with a vow to call back the following morning. Either that, or drive up to the goddamn place himself.

"Hello?"

Holden shot to his feet. "Mother! How are you?"

"Hello, Holden. I'm well."

I'm well? That was oddly . . . formal.

"It's been months since we last spoke. I'm hoping you're more than well. Ecstatic. Extremely busy. Involved in a whirlwind romance with a tortured young psychic from a biker gang."

"Nonsense, Holden. It's wrong to suggest I would betray your father."

Holden's jaw dropped. "I'm sorry. Who are you and what have you done with Jessie Payne? You know, the lady who birthed me and gave me my sense of humor and sarcasm?"

"It's fine to have a sense of humor and sarcasm," she said in the same vacantly . . . calm voice. Like a telemarketer. Or the DJ on an easy-listening station. "But I've come to realize sarcasm is often used as a tool to defend myself when I feel insecure. A tool that makes others uncomfortable. And jokes are a weapon to break tension, but they serve only to make people nervous. Your joke about infidelity made me very nervous, Holden."

"Mother. What the fuck?"

"You shouldn't swear," she said. "People may misunderstand and believe your father raised you without respect. I wish you would think before speaking."

This was surreal. More than surreal. It was completely incomprehensible even as a nightmare. There had never been a point in Holden's life when he'd expected his mother, the crass young psychic from Shirley, Long Island, to be lecturing him on Stepford manners and appearances. She'd been the one to initiate the infidelity jokes back when he was a preteen. Back when they'd come to realize they were both involved in a loveless relationship with Richard Payne, whose primary concern had always been with the Community.

"I'm going to pretend you don't sound like a pod person," he said slowly, "and get right to the meat of why I called."

"To wish me happy holidays," she said like a very warm robot on a mission to make apple pie. "How lovely."

"No. Not so lovely. I'm calling to ask if you've heard anything on that end about the fallout from the Beck situation. It seems like the board has people investigating everyone who spent time around her, and I'm starting to worry—"

"Holden . . ."

She sounded so strange. First mellow like one of those guitarists who sat in Union Square all day, and now strained.

"What's wrong?"

"Holden."

"Mother, I don't know what the hell is going on, but I need information. I'm really starting to worry that the Comm is going to cover their asses by blaming me for the disappearances. Why take responsibility for not having checked out one of their inner circle when they could just say me and the other Evo staff are incompetent?" She didn't answer, and he blew out a frustrated breath. "I just want to know what to expect. Are they trying to find out if we were in on it with her, which is ridiculous, or are they—"

"Holden!"

"Mother!" he said in the same tone. "What the hell is going on? You don't sound like yourself."

There was another silence, but this one was punctuated by the start and stop of words. Like she was trying to respond but something was preventing her from finishing a sentence.

"Holden," she finally said, worn-out and defeated. "Please take care."

The call ended.

The Farm was a sort of mystery to Holden. He knew its function, but he had no idea how it operated on a day-to-day basis.

As a kid, both his parents had taken him to the Farm during the holidays. They'd have a toy or food drive at the CW along with a large gathering before spending a few days upstate. Later, his father had transitioned it from a family property to a Community space. Even after that transition had begun, Holden mostly remembered it in a positive light.

Psys in need of intense therapy had stayed at the beautiful property, and Holden and his mother had gone there on weekends to check in on how things were running. Well, his mother had checked in while he helped in the kitchen or did another menial job to earn his keep while everyone else did more important things. He'd been enamored by the people who lived and worked on the Farm—people his parents had talked about almost as if they were saints for devoting their lives to others. And, for a time, Holden had wanted to do the same. Until he'd discovered he'd rather devote his life to running after boys.

Later, they'd visited Chase there. He'd always been such an enigma. Instead of running around happily like the other children growing up on the Farm, the children whose parents lived there, he was withdrawn with shifty eyes and a vacant stare.

After Chase moved to the city, Holden's memories of the place became colored by the resentment of his adolescence, when he'd been remanded to the rambling property for realignment after doing something particularly embarrassing. In most cases, it had been something particularly gay. Fucking the wrong person's son or getting caught with his pants down at the wrong event. His biggest offense had been at the annual member gala one year—a black-tie affair where members had gathered to discuss the year's accomplishments and future goals. Seriously pointless since it always amounted to upper-tier psychics patting themselves on the backs about how far the Comm had come in only a couple of decades. So Holden had dipped out . . . with a friend. And they'd been caught jerking each other off in the coatroom.

His father's henchmen had dragged him off kicking and screaming. He'd sulked the entire car ride up to the Farm, and had cursed every human to interact with him during the first few days of his stay. At the time, he'd seen it as an incarceration. After all, he'd been remanded to a room with locked doors in one of the three houses on the property while tutors and Comm counselors came to him in turn. He'd been a prisoner.

But had it really been as dramatic as that? Hadn't they given him nutritious gourmet meals and a comfortable bed? Hadn't the grounds been well-kept and beautiful? Or was that just what they'd fed into his head over the weeks and months he was there until he'd internalized it? It was hard to say, so his paranoid thoughts about the strange phone call with his mother were probably unfounded. And yet they persisted through the rest of the night.

He was supposed to be a judge for the costume contest, but all he could think about was his mother. Her voice had been alien and her personality not her own. No quick wit or the sharp tongue he'd inherited. The self-deprecating side of her that came out when she was depressed or anxious hadn't even reared up. She'd just been a vessel repeating overprotective nonsense about his father and the Community. It made no sense unless she'd been brainwashed or unless . . . someone had been listening.

Holden's attention strayed from the current contestant in the costume contest—a young man in glittery red leggings and a bow over his crotch—and found Six in the crowd. As usual, he lingered at the back like a sentinel. Blank, silent, and slightly menacing with his ripped muscles and tattoos. Several patrons had so far admitted being both frightened and attracted to him. Holden could relate. Although right now he wasn't worried about Six's lumbersexual qualities. He was more interested in what the man knew about the Farm.

Across the crowd, Six stopped glaring at a throuple trying to get out onto the patio and turned to meet Holden's eyes. It was almost like he could sense the weight of Holden's stare. He looked up to catch

Holden watching him almost every single time. *Eerie* didn't begin to describe it.

"Mr. Payne?"

Holden jerked out of his reverie and realized two hundred people were staring at him and waiting for him to judge a costume. He frowned, eyeballing the leggings again, and came to the quick conclusion that there was no way he'd be able to concentrate on the absurdity of this event. Not while his brain was going wild with conspiracy theories.

"Sorry, I need to make a phone call." Holden ignored the look of disappointment on Elf Boy's face. He was vaguely recognizable as a third-rate precog who read palms in Greenwich Village between classes at NYU. "Kamryn, can you take over for me?"

Kamryn looked like she'd rather swallow her own tongue, but she pasted on a fake smile and climbed up on the tiny stage. "Suuure."

"Thanks, love. I owe you." Holden squeezed her shoulder and then slapped Elf Boy's ass. "Nice tights."

The crowd hooted as Holden hopped off the stage and pushed through the swarm of bodies. They pressed in on each other with no regard for personal space. By the time he was face-to-face with Six, Holden was almost positive he was covered in glitter or sequins from the various costumes.

"Do you hit on everyone who comes through that door?"

Holden arched an eyebrow. "Does it bother you?"

"No. It just makes you look like a jackass."

"Well, don't sugarcoat it or anything."

Six went back to scanning the crowd. "People would take you more seriously if you weren't such a horndog."

"That's nice, Sixtus. Unfortunately, I don't take advice from virgins." Holden put his hand on one of Six's big shoulders and guided him backward. "We need to talk."

Six grabbed Holden's wrist and squeezed so hard he swore something crunched. "Don't touch me unless I ask you to."

"Nice phrasing." It was tempting to touch him again, but Holden wasn't convinced extensive teasing wouldn't result in him having broken bones. "Can we have a normal discussion now?"

"What about? You see I'm working, right?"

"I see you trying to glare various costume-clad queers into submission. But this is serious." Six looked at him without comment, and Holden sighed. "Listen, I need to talk to you about the Farm. Please?"

Just like earlier, the *p*-word cracked Six's hard-ass exterior. Holden wondered if that was all it took to get Six to comply. Without a way for Six to gauge emotions or mood, it was probably difficult to tell whether a sarcastic bastard like Holden was serious or not.

"Let's go to the patio."

Holden cut his way through the crowd. Just like before, people grabbed for him along the way. More than one called out a compliment or an invitation.

"They act like you're a rock star," Six noted once they were outside again. "No wonder you're so arrogant."

"Oh please. I was born arrogant. And they only give a damn about me because of my last name."

"It's true, but I didn't expect you to admit it."

"Yes, it's very clear you think little of me." Holden tried not to take that personally. It was easier since he had bigger fish to fry. "I need information about the Farm, and you're the only person I can ask."

"Why don't you ask your father?"

"Because my father doesn't trust me." *And I don't trust him.* "And he isn't there on a regular basis. You were."

"As a guard." Six leaned against the door with his arms crossed over his chest. "I have no insight as to how decisions are made about the psys who are held there. I provided security for the facility. That's it."

"But that's what I need to know about."

"And you think I'll discuss it with you?" The combination of beard, man bun, and cocked brow made Sixtus look like a condescending hipster. "You may be Richard Payne's son, but you're not a staff member. Especially not on the Farm, which is far more secure than the CW."

"Why's that?"

"Because the Farm is off-limits to anyone in the outside world. The CW is a front."

A front. All of these years, Holden had known it had a double purpose, but no one had ever referred to it as . . . a front. A front for what, though? They did take in displaced psychics and guide them. He'd seen it himself. He'd even volunteered there as a kid.

"So you're telling me you're unable to give me information about the Farm's security, the conditions under which people are held, and even how people live?"

"Correct."

"So, for example, you can't tell me if, for some reason, residents are . . . closely monitored."

Six tilted his head against the door and regarded Holden from beneath his long lashes. "Do you have a theory you're trying to confirm, or are you just spit-balling?"

"Are you going to turn around and report my theories to my father?"

"Would you trust me even if I said that I wouldn't?"

"Good point." Holden searched Six's face for a long moment before sliding closer and bracing his hands on the door on either side of Six. He smiled. "What if we traded?"

Again, Six just stared at him. This beautiful personification of blankness but with burning black eyes.

"What if you answer one measly little question, and I give you something good in return?"

"Money?"

"I was thinking more along the lines of sex."

"I'd prefer money."

Holden clenched his jaw. It wasn't every day he was flat-out rejected, especially by a cyborg. It was putting a serious cramp in his game.

"You admitted you're a virgin."

"I didn't admit a fucking thing," Six said.

"But you didn't deny it." Holden leaned closer. Six's eyes flicked down to his mouth and back up again. "I could show you what you've been missing."

"Sounds like a bad idea."

"That's because you haven't had someone else get you off before." It was the perfect time to take Six off guard with a kiss, but Holden hesitated. He'd seduced dozens of men in the past twenty years of being sexually active, and this was the first time he was nervous about it. His stomach had never knotted up while his breath caught right before a little peck on the lips. But, then again, all those times he'd reached out with his gift to make sure the other person was into it. He'd *felt* their lust. And Six projected nothing. "Have you ever kissed anyone before, Sixtus?"

Six dropped his big hands onto Holden's shoulders, but he didn't push him away. "You need to back up."

"If you wanted me to back up, you would have shoved me by now. I think you're intrigued."

"Think you can manipulate me with sex." Six laughed dryly, but it sounded forced. "Your father warned me you would try this. He said you're a player. Someone who uses his charm and looks to con people into doing what he wants. And uses his empath skills to finish the job. But none of it works on me."

"How do you know I want to manipulate you?" Six's grip on his shoulders tightened hard enough to be painful, but Holden didn't back off. He moved so close their chests were pressed together. "Maybe I'm just curious as to how you'd react to having my tongue in your mouth. Or your dick in mine." Holden ran his fingers along Six's cheekbone. Six started, clearly unprepared for the light touch. "I bet you have interesting fantasies."

"I do," Six said, but his voice was lower. "You don't speak in them, though."

"We can find a fun way to shut me up right now."

Holden pressed their lips together before he could back off this plan. He half expected to be shoved away and for a fist to crash into his face right before the taste of iron bloomed in his mouth, but it didn't happen. The hands gripping him closed down harder, grinding bone and muscle, but that was the only way Six reacted. At first.

He was initially frozen when their lips brushed, but after one gentle swipe of Holden's tongue, Six opened his mouth. Shuddering, Holden licked into the wet warmth deeper and more insistently.

A groan muffled against him, low and quickly aborted, but Holden heard it. And he felt the way Six leaned into him. It was barely a response, but it encouraged Holden to pin Six against the door and dive into a hungry kiss. This time, Six was an active participant. Their slicking tongues, frantically moving lips, and a full-body press made it quite clear that Six was into this. His dick was fully rocked up in a way that could not be explained by anything other than arousal for Holden.

And Holden was just as hard for him. In fact, his body was reacting in a way it never had before. Every sense was alight as he moved his hands over Six in an effort to feel everything he could. With no impressions to absorb, all he could do was touch.

It was right about the time triumph usually exploded in Holden's chest with invisible banners and balloons celebrating a conquest, but this time he felt apprehension. He didn't want to end this kiss. He wanted Six to keep exploring the inside of his mouth with a delightfully frantic lack of finesse, and he wanted a genuine fucking smile once they were done. But that wasn't in the cards. That wasn't what this was about.

Holden pulled away with a ragged sigh. "I'm guessing you enjoyed your first kiss."

"I never confirmed it was my first," Six said hoarsely. He licked his lips. "You assumed."

"I assume right. I may not be able to read your emotions, but I could feel your heart beating out of your chest."

"And I could feel yours."

He could probably still feel it, because Holden's body was betraying him and his plan by behaving like a giddy schoolboy.

"You liked it," Holden said knowingly. He brushed their lips together again, and smiled when Six immediately leaned in for a deeper kiss. One touch and he was hooked? It couldn't be that easy. Not with him. "And it doesn't take a psychic to know you want more."

"Maybe I'm just curious. It's been thirty years."

"That's a long time to go untouched," Holden agreed. "And, like I said, I can help you out with that. If you help me out with some answers."

The little bit of life that had lit Six's expression immediately vanished. Almost as if he'd forgotten why they'd been kissing, and the words were a wake-up call Holden hadn't expected him to need. Regret slammed into Holden, but he dismissed it with a shake of his head. No matter how good Six felt against him, or how delicious those frantic unpracticed kisses had been, this wasn't about seduction or attraction or intrigue. This was about his mother, the Farm, and whatever the hell the Community had planned for him. Wherever they were keeping Chase.

The fact that Six had been planted here by the people currently trying to pin the recent disasters on Holden mopped up any lingering traces of his reluctance to keep this all business.

"Tell me about the Farm, and I'll let you play out your every fantasy on my body." Holden ran his hand along Six's face, stroking his thick dark whiskers and marveling at how soft his hair was. "As long as you give me what I need."

"And you're going to give me what I need?"

"Yes. No matter how dark or dirty or rough, I'm there for it."

Holden tried not to be affected by the mental images popping into his mind, but it was impossible. Even though Six had defaulted to cyborg mode, there were things about him that Holden couldn't help but notice now. The smell of musk and sweat from working the club all night, the way his fingers flexed, his steady heartbeat, and the fact that Holden could not detect a hint of color in those eyes even at this proximity. Just gleaming black pools that gave nothing away.

"Fine," Six said. "I'll tell you this much—the Farm is the most secure Community facility for a reason. The people held there are considered a risk to the Community, whether that means the folks in charge are worried about them exposing us by being too blatant about their abilities, going to the media for monetary reasons, exposing the Community for some wrongdoing, or even breaking off from the Community."

"How is that a risk? We're free to go at will, just as we were free to join."

"No one is free to join or go," Six said. "Once you're on their radar, you don't leave it. They track every psy they come across. And if you sign the dotted line and try to leave, they try to talk you out of it because now you know Comm secrets. Can't have that, can we? Better keep you on the Farm for a couple of months to try to talk you out of it."

"And how do they do that?"

"By telling you how great the Community is every day, all day, for however long it takes to get you to change your mind." Six's lip lifted into something resembling a smile. "It's very effective. Don't you see how well it worked on me?"

That had to be a trap. The question dripped sarcasm, but Holden didn't believe for a second that Six was really this disparaging about the Community he had been serving for the past couple of decades. Not only was he staff, as he'd called it, but he was security. Oversight. For Richard Payne's son. You didn't get that far without earning some serious trust. Which meant doing or covering up some serious dirt.

Holden nodded without engaging with the question. "During that time are people closely monitored when interacting with the outside world?"

Six laughed dryly.

"What?"

"I just think it's funny how oblivious you are to how this all works."

"I don't find it funny that you're incapable of giving me an answer without mocking me. I'd think you, who appreciates directness, would be better than that."

"I'm being as direct as I can be." Six exhaled slowly, his breath warm and smelling like peppermint. "Yes, *guests* on the Farm are monitored. Closely. So are phone calls. And cells aren't permitted once realignment has started."

"I've experienced realignment before, and I wasn't treated that way."

"Because you were primarily there as a punishment from your father. Real realignment has different levels, but most people get the same treatment. And most people agree to it beforehand."

Had his mother agreed to this level of realignment? It was entirely possible. She'd left the city to go to the Farm because her negative feelings about Holden's father had begun turning into negative feelings about the Community, and that had activated guilt and self-loathing that had been catastrophic for her. She'd hoped the distance from Richard and closeness to the Comm would help, but the change in her personality spelled out a hint to something else happening. Something besides her volunteering to help supervise the place.

Had her distrust and negativity not dissipated, and she'd signed up for realignment as a result? And did realignment turn people into shells of their former selves?

There were too many questions, and he couldn't ask Six any of them. Because then it would be obvious that *he* didn't trust the Community. Maybe then it would be his turn to get shipped off to the Farm.

"Thank you, Sixtus." Holden set his concerns aside and forced a smile, moving his hands down to rub over Six's pecs. His chest was rock-hard and indicative of a serious dedication to working out. "When do you want to meet up?"

"To fuck?"

"Yes. To fuck."

Six looked at him for a long moment before sidestepping him. "I'll pass."

CHAPTER FIVE

"We still don't know anything about Chase?"

"No, but I'm beginning to think he's at the Farm."

Elijah plopped down on an ancient orange recliner, the fabric covered with patches and stitches from years of being ripped open and sewn back together. It was so big that he looked smaller than usual curled up on it, his knees drawn up to his chin and arms wrapped around them. With his tattered cardigan draping around him and a Charlie Brown Christmas tree limply sitting on a side table nearby, he looked like a character in a Dickens novel.

A Dickens novel where the orphans drank whiskey with Pop-Tarts while watching holiday cartoons—a grim reminder that it was Christmas Day, and Holden hadn't even noticed before now. He usually spent the morning with his father at the CW and the evening at the club, but that hadn't even come up. It was painfully obvious that his father was avoiding him. Maybe doing damage control to his own rep if the other founders were wary of Holden and Evo.

It stung, and Holden hated the burn. Why couldn't he be like Elijah, who'd been run out of his own house as a teen and had survived? Or Six, who had flatly told him he'd be spending the day working out and gave no fucks about family or holidays? Why was he so hurt that neither parent had contacted him? Although . . . who knew what was going on with his mother. The memory of that phone call put everything back into perspective.

"Do you think he's there because he wants to be?" Elijah asked, poking at his frosted Pop-Tart. "Like, do you think he's celebrating Christmas or . . . doing some weird group therapy indoctrination about following Community protocol?"

"I couldn't say, Elijah. Did you usually spend the day with him?"

"Yes. And I just want him to be happy. Or at least not . . . entirely miserable." Elijah buried his face in his knees again. He was so out of place in the hodgepodge apartment. *Eclectic* didn't begin to describe it. Paintings and prints covered every available space on the walls along with rows of bookshelves. It was much smaller than Elijah's past apartment, and the belongings weren't his. Apparently, Airbnbs came in handy for people on the run. The clutter was not ideal for an empath, but luckily Holden's mental shield was strong enough to block the vibes. Nate Black wouldn't have been as fortunate. "I went to the Farm when I first joined, but I honestly don't remember a lot about what happened there. I'm pretty sure they're not big into holidays though."

"Wasn't that only a few years ago?"

"Yeah, but it's like the memories are gone." He spread his fingers like an explosion. "Poof."

"Why were you even there?"

Elijah tore at the rip in the knee of his pants. "When they found me, I was drinking and taking pills. They wanted me detoxed and aligned before trusting me to learn everything else about the Comm, I guess."

The running themes of trust and making sure people wouldn't expose the Community were starting to niggle at Holden. There seemed to be more of a focus on keeping things hushed up than truly helping the people they'd originally vowed to protect.

"I wonder what happens to people who, in their eyes, might now or have in the past posed a threat to the Community. Whether it's a real threat or imagined in the minds of the board members. Or just fear. That would be even worse—the idea that they're letting fear drive their actions." Holden sat on the edge of a similarly overstuffed chair with a colorful checkered pattern. "I'm starting to wonder if a lot of people who go to the Farm long-term end up sounding like puppets like my mother or disappear into some portal like Chase?"

"Don't say it like that. Please." Elijah closed his eyes. "It makes it sound like we'll never see him again."

"How do we know we will? How do I know I'll see my mother?"

"How do you know we won't?" Elijah demanded, abruptly sitting upright. He kicked his legs out in front of him and slid to the edge of the cushion. "I know this all looks bad, but I want to believe he'll be okay. Maybe he's just going through realignment because he tried to figure out the Beck thing on his own instead of going to your father? I'm sure it doesn't help that he brought an outsider into it." Elijah hunched forward, cracking his knuckles and looking imploringly up at Holden. "Think about it. Even if Nate is psy, he still isn't part of the Comm. And I'm pretty sure he never wants to be. At this point, I don't want to be either. I wish I'd never gotten sucked into all of this bullshit. It's starting to feel like . . . a giant scam to get money from members in exchange for control over our actions and undying loyalty. What do we even get in return?"

Even knowing there was something suspicious going on, the words hurt. Without the Comm, Holden would have never met Elijah. Besides that, Elijah was one of the people the Community had truly come through for, which was why he had a testimonial on a plaque at the CW. There were dual parts of Holden's brain warring about whether he should let the comments slide or point this out and defend the Community.

Holden opened his mouth to go for something in the middle, to point out that all of this drama and confusion was likely due to nothing this bad having ever happened in the Comm before, and now the leaders were overreacting due to panic. But words of defense wouldn't come with his own father allowing blame to be laid at his feet. But believing in something for so many years only to have it fall apart bit by bit felt like a knife twisting in his gut.

Holden blew out a slow breath, sorting through everything Elijah had said. "It's possible he's going through realignment, but it works differently for different people. I had a light version when I was a kid, but that likely has more to do with my father than anyone else. The only person I can think of who has been thoroughly subjected to the full treatment is Sixtus, and asking him is out of the question."

Especially since they'd been avoiding each other for the past couple of days. Six had even stopped gracing him with his blunt observations and dry sarcasm. He kept his distance. They'd only exchanged words when Holden had awkwardly asked about holiday plans.

"What reason did your father give for sending Sixtus?" Elijah asked, voice lowering as if Six would be able to hear it from uptown. "Just another person to keep an eye on the club, or did he finally admit that he wants someone keeping an eye on *you*?"

"We all know he wants me to have a handler, but I'm starting to think I finally know the real reason why . . ." Now Holden was copying Elijah and lowering his voice with every word. "They know they fucked up with Beck, and there's apparently discontent in the Community. Maybe even with the board. Apparently, the only way they can think of to cover their asses is to put the blame on us for not spotting Beck sooner. Which means I absolutely do not trust Six. He was the one who told me the deal, but that doesn't mean anything. He was sent by my father. And apparently he isn't the only one."

Elijah shrank in on himself again. "You're talking about those guys who've been following me."

"So you knew."

"Of course I knew. I'm not an idiot."

"I didn't mean to imply you were. I just didn't know if they ever made their presence known more overtly."

"They're the same guys who showed up at Lia's house to look for me." Elijah glanced at his phone. "And, speaking of Lia, she's going to be here in a few minutes."

"Oh. I didn't realize you were having company."

Holden started to stand, but Elijah shook his head. "She wants to talk to you."

"About?"

Elijah bit his lower lip and glanced at the door. "All of this."

"What do you mean . . . 'all of this'?" Holden's brow crashed down. "Fuck, Elijah, you didn't run your mouth about Community shit to Lia, did you? That is absolutely unacceptable."

"'Unacceptable'? Seriously?" Elijah got to his feet and put his hands on his hips. "After all that's happened, and all that's going on, you expect me to care about rules made up by people like your father? Rich psychics who use their influence to turn us into puppets?"

Those dual urges reared up again, but instead of fighting them, Holden took a step forward. "Where is this coming from, Elijah? I know what happened with Beck was awful. I may not have been as close with Jericho or Theo as you were, but I cared about them both. Especially Theo. And I hate that it happened under my nose. I hate that the Community is trying to cover up their own oversight, but that doesn't change that they *helped* you. *I* have helped you. And six months ago, you were one of the Community's biggest cheerleaders. You were one of the main people railing against Theo when he started throwing the Comm under the bus!"

"I know that," Elijah said, voice lowering. "And I feel awful for it now."

"Okay. I'll ask again. *Where is this coming from*?"

"It's coming from me wondering if I was their biggest cheerleader because . . ." Elijah's dark eyes flashed damply. He crossed his arms over his chest. "Because they knew how to manipulate a gay kid with no family. They knew I would do anything to be accepted somewhere, so they found my weaknesses and exploited them. Had me thinking the Community was basically my church and you and your dad were my gods for saving me. And had me feeling so grateful and indebted that I never questioned the membership fee, the rules, or the idea that turning on your friends like I did to Theo was for their own sake and for a greater good of the Community." Elijah swallowed heavily, hugging himself tighter. "And there's so many Comm members like me, Holden. It's almost like they seek out people who are missing something in their lives . . . so they can fill the holes and leave us feeling terrified of losing the organization that saved us."

Holden didn't know what to say. Especially because . . . it rang true. And similar thoughts had drifted through his own head after his father had gone along with him opening Evolution. He'd wondered if Richard had wanted him to collect more kids like Elijah. The lost always became the most loyal.

But those weren't things he was prepared to say out loud.

A knock on the door served as both an interruption and Holden's answer. He pursed his lips and watched Elijah edge around him to answer the door.

Lia walked in wrapped in a leather bomber jacket, multiple scarves, and boots that consumed her entire leg and half of her thigh.

She'd bleached and cut her hair, and she looked glamorous even as her eyes skewered Holden to the spot as soon as they set on him.

"Long time no see, Payne."

"Same. How is your holiday going?"

"I'm an atheist."

"Oh. Sorry for assuming."

Lia snorted and unwound one of her scarves. "Listen, I don't want to be rude, but we need to talk, and I'm running on limited time."

"It depends on what we're talking about," he countered. "If it's about the situation with people following Elijah to your house, I would love to figure out why that's happening. If it's about the Community being a big bad organization who wants to turn us all into puppets . . . Well . . . I may be less agreeable."

Lia exchanged looks with Elijah before swinging a much less impressed gaze back to his face. "So you're still drinking your daddy's Kool-Aid."

"Actually, I'm not. I know something isn't right. I'm not an idiot. But I also refuse to drink *your* Kool-Aid and tell myself that they've never done anything good for anybody. I've seen the results of what they can do—and Elijah is an example of that and so is my brother. So are a lot of the other gay kids I've hired on at the club."

"That's your mistake, Holden. That's not the Community making a difference. It's you." Lia unwound the second scarf and let them dangle from her hand. "You're being defensive because you think you've seen evidence of the fruits of their labor, but the labor was yours. You took Elijah in. You treated Chase like your brother. You hand selected troubled and homeless psys to work at Evolution. Not your daddy. Not Lukas Kyger or Michelle Hale. You."

The statement took the wind out of Holden's defensive sails. "I'm not the only one who's helped. Community Watch is—"

"The board doesn't run Community Watch by themselves. They put people there to run it, so yeah, there have been great success stories. People who've been nurtured and then sent out into the world to get jobs at companies run by successful psychics, and they use their new salaries to pay their annual Community membership fees. Lifetime membership fees." Lia swung her scarf back and forth like a pendulum. "And then the even more successful psychics, the ones they found young and put through school—the ones with charisma and high intellect . . . Well, those guys go into policy making. They get federal jobs. Sometimes even Department of Justice or Defense. Sometimes Congress. Sometimes they go even higher than that."

"I'm sorry, but are you suggesting . . ." Holden tried to keep the skeptically smart-ass look off his face and failed. "Are you implying the Community exists to make money off members in some cases and use them as . . . pawns in others?"

"Yes. That's exactly what I'm saying. And I'm not the only one who feels that way." Lia's expression didn't flicker. She didn't stop swinging her scarf. "There's an entire group of people who feel just like me."

"Really."

"Really," she said. "Ex-Community members and psychics who've been warned to stay away. Jericho was in that group, and that's why he's dead. I strongly believe that."

"Jericho's dead because he knew too much about Beck and what she was up to. Or at least she must have thought so to have felt the need to silence him."

"Right. Beck." Lia stopped swinging the scarf and balled it in her hand. "Beck, whose known gift was spotting rare and multitalented psychics. That's who your father planted in Evolution to watch you. Not another empath, or an invulnerable like Six who won't be swayed—"

Holden's eyes narrowed. "How do you know—"

"—not a postcog who could've helped you to figure out why people were disappearing, or a precog who could have helped you avoid future problems. He put in . . . a spotter. And that makes sense to you."

Elijah was starting to look uneasy at the direction the conversation was going in. He wrung his hands together, shifting from foot to foot, but didn't interrupt. He'd probably heard all this before. Maybe he even believed it. Whatever *it* was. That Holden's father had wanted Beck to find rare talents for him?

"You can't believe he wanted her to go around eating psychic powers."

"Not necessarily, but you bet your sweet ass I believe the board is constantly looking for new pawns to turn into loyal drones who can be strategically placed. Maybe they didn't expect Beck to go Hannibal on them, but it's their fault she was there. I mean, fuck, are we even sure she killed them all? Maybe a couple got swooped up beforehand and sent up to the Farm like Chase. For realignment." Lia shrugged. "Either way, Beck wasn't acting on her own. It's all part of the bigger picture, Holden. And the only reason I'm telling you this is because Elijah told me to trust you. He's seen you working with Ex-Comm, and he believes we need you."

Holden's jaw dropped. There were clearly no half measures for Lia. She was going all the way in with this conspiracy theory, and apparently Elijah was right there with her. The fact that she knew so much about the Community, about the Farm and realignment and his father, made it clear someone had been talking.

"Elijah, what the fuck?"

Elijah wrapped his cardigan tighter around him. "Yeah, I sort of had a vision . . . about us. And you. And Nate . . ."

"Doing *what*?"

"We were all together in this wooded area. By a river or a lake or something." Elijah's eyes grew far away as he talked about it. The typically vivid color faded and turned foggy, a haze that indicated he really was seeing the future. A future in which they reunited with Nate. "I can't see anything else. My gift has never been that strong, but . . . it's also never been this clear. We were all together, and we were with Nate."

"And you didn't think to tell me any of this before?"

"Lia explains things better than me. And I've only just learned about Ex-Comm."

"'Ex-Comm,'" Holden repeated. "Is that your little anti-Community group?"

"Yes," Lia said. "Although it's not so little anymore."

Holden glared at her, and Elijah rushed over to touch his arm.

"Holden, even if you don't believe us now, I know you will at some point. I have no doubt that you'll be right here with us trying to figure out what the Community *really* wants from us all, and how

Beck, Jericho, Theo, and all the others fit into that plan. How Chase and your mother are fitting into it now."

When Holden said nothing, Lia picked up the slack. Her voice softened, although there was still an edge of *get your shit together* in her tone.

"The organization raised you. I get it. I get that it's hard to open your eyes to the fact that it isn't what you've thought it is, but it's time. People have been hurt. They've been fucking killed. And it's not just Evolution that was targeted." Lia hesitated for a moment, maybe wondering if she could trust him with whatever else she was thinking about, before saying, "Ex-Comm was formed by people who escaped after being manipulated or mistreated by Community staff, but it's populated by both psys and voids who have had extremely talented family members disappear after coming into contact with the Comm. It's not just Evolution, Holden. It wasn't just Beck. She let her own resentment and bitterness turn her into a monster, but I have no fucking doubts that she was placed there for the sole purpose of snapping up rare psychics. Those disappearances would have happened had she cannibalized them or not."

"Well maybe you should have doubts, because this is on another level of ludicrous."

Holden pulled away from Elijah and grabbed his coat from the side of the recliner and yanked it on. He was running away, and he didn't care. Fight-or-flight instincts were kicking in, and they were telling him to get the fuck out of this tiny studio. Away from Lia and Elijah. Back to Hell's Kitchen. It didn't help that when he reached out with his talent, he felt that they one hundred percent believed what they were saying. And Elijah had really seen that vision. Which only made him want to run even farther and faster.

"Holden, don't go."

Elijah reached for him, but Lia stepped between them.

"Let him leave. He isn't ready."

"I'll never be ready for this nonsense. Call me when you want to talk about something real."

It was colder when Holden returned to Manhattan. The wind cut through his clothes and skin to chill his bones, and yet he didn't return to his apartment or Evolution. He kept walking past Ninth Avenue, then Tenth, until he was striding into the increasingly desolate streets that ran into the West Side Highway and the Hudson River.

Holden ducked his head, hands shoved into the pockets of his wool coat, and kept walking. Without purpose at first, but then something deep inside of him began tugging him to a specific street and a specific pier. A pier that sent dark vibes snaking through him with the speed of a spreading ice as soon as he stopped in front of the makeshift memorial for Theo Black. Even after six months, it was intact.

Kneeling beside it, Holden ran his fingers along the dying roses and weathered cards. The flowers were new enough to have been placed there within the last week, which meant someone still cared. Maybe Lia and Elijah. Or someone else Theo had made a connection with who had nothing to do with Evolution or the Community. Someone completely uninvolved in the brewing shit-storm, and who had no idea that Theo's death had started a downward spiral for both Comm leaders and members alike. Trust was at an all-time low among the psychics who came to Evolution, with everyone so desperate to explain what had happened that they were willing to point fingers and come up with wild theories.

But . . . was Lia's theory so wild?

Holden sat on the cold pier with his legs folded under him and his head in his hands.

He wished Chase was with him. Throughout their childhood, Chase had always been the fearless one. The one who wasn't afraid to take matters into his own hands and then convey his findings with brutal honesty. Holden had never been able to tell if his half brother didn't care about being sensitive and careful, or if he'd simply been born without those attributes in exchange for the multiple extrasensory abilities he *had* likely inherited from the Blacks. He'd always been special. And, yet, he hated that about himself. Chase often called himself a mutant and a freak, and wished he was normal.

Holden had never understood why Chase had such self-loathing for his own gifts, why he'd sometimes told Holden to not talk about it around the Payne family or prominent members of the Community. It had almost been like he'd wanted to hide it, or himself, but Holden had never known why.

If Lia was right, maybe he'd wanted to avoid becoming one of the people that spotters . . . collected and used as pawns. Or maybe he'd been afraid of other psychic vampires like Beck.

Maybe that was why he'd kept the truth about Beck to himself. And why he'd reached out to another Black instead of the brother who'd been at his side all along.

The reality that Chase hadn't trusted him hit Holden like a punch in the gut.

"You look homeless."

Holden jerked to awareness so abruptly that his neck spasmed as he looked up. Six was looming over him in a pair of sweatpants and a hoodie. He wore running shoes and a headband to keep back his man bun.

"And you look like Rocky Balboa goes hipsta-matic. What are you, doing a remake?"

Six didn't crack a smile. "Why are you crying?"

Was he? Jesus. Holden ripped an arm over his face. "I'm not."

"You are. I can see tears on your face. That was a stupid lie."

"You know, Six, this would be an apt time to put those body-language-reading abilities to good use since your mental shield has also blocked off people skills." Holden sniffled and wiped his face again. "For future reference, heckling someone who's trying to hide their tears is generally not the sort of thing normal humans do."

"I'm not a normal human. I'm an invulnerable."

"Oh my God. Forget it." Holden climbed to his feet, wincing. When had his knees become this much of a problem? He blamed the cold instead of his age. "Are you following me?"

"Yes."

Holden froze with his hands poised to brush over his coat. "What?"

"I followed you to Elijah's house. I was jogging now though, so this part is a coincidence. I live in a loft a couple of blocks away."

"Wait. Rewind. Why the hell did you follow me to Elijah's apartment?"

"To see what you were doing."

Holden was going to kill him. He really was. "*Why?*"

"Because you seem emotionally unstable lately, and I wondered where you were going."

"Again—*why?*"

Six shrugged. "I have nothing else to do."

"So you just go around following people?" Holden demanded. "This is not okay."

"Why? Was I not supposed to know you were meeting him?"

"You're not supposed to be fucking following me," Holden shouted, his voice carrying over the water. "Did my father put you up to this?"

"No." Six scanned the area around them. With the exception of the cars speeding along the highway, there appeared to be nobody around for blocks. And yet he kept looking. "Let's just say I wanted to make sure I'm the only one who was sent to keep an eye on you."

Holden stopped wanting to throttle Six long enough to look at him sideways. "Excuse me?"

"I was given a job. That job was to keep you and your stupid club out of trouble." Six stopped analyzing the desolate streets to meet Holden's confused gaze. "Which means there should be no other Community thugs following you around the way they do your friends. You feel me?"

"I . . . No. I don't." Holden shook his head. "So you're saying you followed me . . . to make sure nobody else was following me?"

"Yeah. Thanks for catching up."

Holden flipped him off. "Your logic is completely off."

"Maybe, but that's how I operate."

"What would you have done if you'd found out someone else was following me?"

"I would have found out why."

"And would you have told me?"

Six started walking backward. "Yes."

There was no reason in the world why Holden should have believed Six, but for some reason . . . he did.

"Let's go," Six said, turning. "It's cold."

"Where are we going?"

"To get something to eat."

It was the most unexpected invitation Holden had ever received, but he took it without a second thought.

CHAPTER SIX

They walked up to Eleventh Avenue through the increasingly cold wind until Six silently led him to a place between Forty-fourth and Forty-third streets. There was an empty lot on the spot with a gate around it and the beginning signs of construction.

"I mean, I guess it's possible that the construction workers would have been here on Christmas to share their sandwiches . . ."

Six gave him a cold look. "There used to be a diner here. It was my favorite place to eat."

"Welp, now it's being turned into . . ." Holden squinted at the sign on the gate. "A high-rise apartment building."

In an uncharacteristic show of absolute sullen irritation, Six kicked the gate. "Fucking New York. This shit always happens."

"What always happens?"

"They tear everything down to make way for chain stores or condos. This place had real character," Six said, pointing at the empty lot. "It was here for decades. Rat Pack era. The Westies used to go there."

"The who?"

Six glared. "Where is your family from, man?"

"The Paynes have been in Manhattan since the turn of the century."

"What *part* of Manhattan?"

"Upper East Side."

"Then you do not count."

"How nice of you." This was sort of amusing, and a nice distraction from the emo mess Holden had been not even ten minutes ago. Who knew real estate in NYC was what really got Sixtus going? "Now tell me what a Westie is."

"It's an Irish American gang that ran Hell's Kitchen until the nineties. But it doesn't matter. Clearly everything from that era will be bulldozed to make way for twenty-year-olds from out of town." Six kicked the gate again. "This used to be my favorite spot."

"When?"

"Before I went to the Farm, I'd scrap for money and get dinner here. Over a decade ago."

"A *decade* ago?" Holden demanded. "They had you upstate for that long?"

"Yes. I was upstate for most of the past fifteen years and worked there for about ten."

"Christ. No wonder you're a virgin with no social skills."

Six's eyes narrowed. "What happened to your hypothesis about me just being a cyborg with no empathy?"

"Do you really have no empathy? I can't tell if it's *really* blocked because of your mental shield or if you're just . . . an asshole."

Six kept giving him the same irritated look. "My shield is so strong that I can't remove it, and it blocks out everything. Most people can tell when someone is tense or annoyed even without psychic powers. But I can't. At all. It's the same reason why I have difficulties with sarcasm. And jokes. And why my social life is lacking."

"I'd say being forced to work at an isolated farm as a goddamn security guard for ten years would have more of an impact on your social life."

"Heh. You just might be right."

They went back to staring at the lot, and Holden's mind returned to his father. He'd taken Six off a ten-year stint on the Farm to babysit Holden. Regardless of whether Six was really invested in the assignment or if he knew anything more than what he'd been told, he was still there to keep an eye on Holden.

The relief to be doing and thinking about something other than Elijah and Chase crashed into fiery bits at Holden's feet. There was no way to escape the questions surrounding the Comm and the situation with Beck, because he was constantly reminded that his own father was part of the reason there was so much uncertainty in the first place.

"I don't feel like eating anymore."

"Fine." Six shoved his hands into his pockets, looked Holden up and down, and then started to turn away.

Holden grabbed his shoulder, holding him in place. "Wait."

"What?"

"I wasn't trying to dismiss you from my presence, Sixtus. I just have no appetite." He sensed Six about to yank away and held on tighter. "We could do something else."

"Like what?"

"Go back to my place," Holden said. "Talk. Drink." He licked his chapped lips, wishing he could read Six. With anyone else, he'd be able to dive into that mental space and figure out exactly what they wanted from him. Then he could give it to them, or figure out how to make them want something else. The absence of that ability, that privilege, was putting him on edge. Making him feel more out of control than he'd ever felt before. "Fuck."

Six turned to him again, regarding Holden closely. It was that moment, that hesitation, that let Holden know he had a real shot at Six. Not just fucking him, but getting close to him. Maybe even close enough to earn his trust.

"Fucking you seems to come at a price, and I'm not really in the mood to debate with you about how to pay."

"Did I ask you for anything? The only negotiating I'm interested in right now is trying to convince you that coming home with me would lead to activities a lot more . . . enjoyable than freezing our asses off by the river. Unless . . ." Holden's brows hiked up. "Unless you think my father wouldn't approve of you screwing the person you've been hired to spy on."

Six's mouth twitched.

"And unless you're more worried about his approval than getting laid for the first time since your extended . . . assignment upstate. I guess I could see why the opinion of some dull old rich guy is more important than getting your dick suc—"

"Shut up, Holden."

Holden was almost positive that was the first time Six had said his first name. His stomach went hollow, his heart pounding a little faster. It was a reaction he hadn't experienced in a long time. Not since his childhood crush had first kissed him, nailed him, and then turned out to be interested in nothing more than Holden's psychic abilities and last name. Psy chasers were the worst of the worst, and the mostly void psychics in the Community were ruthless if they thought they could social climb. The hierarchy of the Community had a way of bringing out the worst side of people. Beck was an extreme example in that regard.

"So are we going or what?"

Six turned his dark eyes to the empty lot again. He regarded it, the space where his favorite restaurant used to be before the city had moved ahead and left him behind, and then slowly nodded.

"We're going. And my place is closer."

Six's apartment had absolutely no character. It was the biggest waste of a large loft-style space that Holden had ever seen.

There were gorgeous hardwood floors, exposed bricks, a freight elevator, and high vaulted ceilings. The windows were incredible—floor to ceiling, which allowed for amazing lighting, but little to no furniture for it to shine on. With the exception of a small television with rabbit ear antennas, a rickety-looking futon sitting against the wall, and a mattress on the floor in the farthest corner from the windows, there was nothing in the apartment besides a standing wardrobe. Holden was tempted to look inside of it and see if it contained half skintight T-shirts and half skintight polos bought from Conways—if that place even existed anymore.

Holden stood in the middle of the empty space, looking around in disbelief. "How long have you been here?"

"A couple of weeks," Six said, unzipping his coat.

"I thought you grew up here."

The comment earned him another of those unimpressed stares. "I grew up in the area back before it was overcome with rich yuppies, but not in this particular apartment. Your father gave me the keys to this place when he put me on the assignment at Evolution."

Holden froze for a single moment before scanning every surface of the place. "How do you know there aren't cameras in here?"

"Ha." Six kicked off his sneakers. "You trust your father that little?"

"It never would have occurred to me before, but things are different now." Holden slowly unzipped his own jacket. "And I don't think you'd want him knowing what's about to happen."

"I don't know what's about to happen."

Either this guy had negative one million game or he was playing coy. Something about Six's blank expression and loose body language told Holden he wasn't fooling around. He appeared to have no idea what to expect from Holden now that they were in the apartment together.

"How is it possible that no one has tried to get in your pants?"

"I'm not the most personable human."

"That's for certain," Holden said with a snort. "But you're gorgeous. The combination of your skin color and black hair is gorgeous. If you weren't such an asshole, I could probably get lost in your eyes. They're beautiful."

"A woman at the Farm told me I had devil eyes, and the description got around. For ten years, that was my nickname. Devil Eyes."

"I'm sure it didn't help that you're not . . . personable." Holden crossed the large room to drape his wool coat over the side of the futon. Once there, he also kicked off his shoes. "But I have a hard time believing nobody at the Farm tried to seduce the hot security guard. I'd think you being silent and mysterious would add to the intrigue."

"That's because you've never experienced the real Farm," Six said. "Most people who are there for an extended period of time know better than to try for any fraternizing. They're there for realignment, not to get their rocks off. And trying to fuck around with anyone was a guaranteed way to extend your realignment. It shows lack of investment in the Community and focus."

"Wanting to fuck shows a lack of investment in the Community? That is absolutely absurd."

"I don't disagree, but that is the general belief of the type of people who work at the Farm." Six lifted his sweatshirt over his head and tossed it onto the futon with Holden's jacket. Beneath it, he wore a gray T-shirt that clearly illustrated every line of his torso. "Anyone who volunteers to live there, isolated from the rest of the fucking world, and signs all the confidentiality agreements, is basically a fanatic."

"But not you?"

"I didn't volunteer to be there."

The statement was so loaded that Holden didn't feel he could respond. They weren't nearly close enough to be going down this road. All the questions that sprang to mind made it very clear how little faith he was beginning to have in the Community, and he could not show that much of his doubt to one of his father's employees. Even if he didn't want to believe it was all as terrible as Lia claimed, it was clear there was a growing element within the organization that would do anything possible to protect the integrity of the place. Even if that integrity was a lie.

Holden flashed a smile, hoping it wasn't strained, and stepped closer to Six. With his hands sliding up that hard chest and over those big shoulders, he sort of felt like he was starring in a porn video. It was over-the-top seduction, more effort than he usually put forth when the cards were on the table about where this was going, but he felt the need to ease Six into it. It wasn't like with Stefen—his bouncer— who'd been inexperienced but an open book for Holden to read. Every attempt to get an impression from Six, which Holden found himself doing automatically every now and then, resulted in a faint static shock.

Holden had been with a lot of men who claimed to be straight, but he'd never actually been with a virgin. Not since high school, anyway. If there was a middle ground between wanting to be considerate of someone's first time while also planning to fuck Six into trusting him enough to spill information, Holden hadn't found it.

"Just so we're clear, you *do* want to lose your V card, yes? I'm not nudging an ace guy into something he doesn't really have interest in? Because that's not my style."

Six reacted to the question as much as he was reacting to Holden's hands on him—not at all. Just even breathing and intense staring.

"I'm not asexual."

"So virgin by lack of opportunity."

"Correct."

Holden pulled off his own sweater. He suppressed a shudder once his bare skin was exposed to the cold air in the apartment. There didn't appear to be any heat on, which further fed his theory that Six was at least part cyborg. The man wasn't even shivering.

"Are you gay? Bi? Pan?"

"I'm attracted to both men and women." He had no intonation as he spoke, but in that moment something in Six's demeanor changed. A slight tensing of his body, like he was bracing for a blow, before his gaze flicked to the window and back to Holden's face. "But I haven't felt anything for anyone in a long time."

"No hot psychics at the Farm?"

"No."

"Not once in all those years?"

Six's mouth tightened at the sides before he said, "Not once. Like I said, there was no fraternizing. It wasn't the type of place that allowed you to get close to people. Or notice people in a sexual way."

There was no way Holden believed people at the Farm were so *focused* on their realignment to the Comm that they didn't notice the people around them. Regardless of someone's dedication or faith, people were people. And people craved human interaction, whether it was sexual or simple friendship. Holden could not imagine how living in a place so isolated for an extended time would *not* lead to close connections.

"Are you saying you notice me in a sexual way, Sixtus Rossi? I assumed you were just taking the first proposition to come your way."

"Both." Six paused for half a breath before taking a step closer. Those dark eyes ran over Holden slowly, analyzing every inch of his body, before returning to rest on his face. Cyborg or not, Six couldn't have hidden the heat in his gaze even if he'd tried. Whether he liked Holden as a person or not was up in the air, but there was absolutely no denying that he wanted him. "I noticed your eyes first. You have psy-kid eyes."

"Meaning?"

"Meaning they glow when you try to do your thing. And since your eyes are hazel, they look golden when you extend your gift. Like a hawk."

"That's . . . No one has ever mentioned that before."

"Most people don't notice. They're too busy doing other things to pay attention to a half-second flash of light they'd likely write off as a figment of their imagination."

"But you always pay attention," Holden said. "Or else you can't read people."

"Correct."

Holden slowly nodded. He'd have to take a video of himself reaching out with his gift some time. "What else did you notice?"

Six's lips tilted up. "You fishing for compliments?"

"Absolutely. I love hearing how attractive I am."

"I'm sure you hear it a lot."

"Yes. But not from someone like you."

"Heh." Six took another step closer. "I also noticed that mouth of yours. Never shuts up, but it's fun to look at. Especially when you're nervous and you start licking your lips. That's what really got my attention. That damp sheen on your mouth. I couldn't stop staring even when you were pissing me off."

Six reached up to rub his thumb over Holden's lower lip, and this time there was no hesitation. For all that he claimed to have no experience, his hands were steady. Holden found himself yet again trying to reach out with his gift, to see if Six was nervous, but felt nothing except the physical touch sending heat soaring through his body.

"I kept thinking about it when I got home," Six said, voice getting huskier. "Was the first time I'd gotten hard thinking about a real person in a long-ass time."

Holden's heart skipped a beat. "What do you usually think about?"

"No one in particular. I usually just jerk off if I'm too tense to sleep."

God, but Holden would pay to watch his cyborg jerk off. Slumped in a chair or spread open on a bed, meat in his hand as he slowly lost control.

"Are you trying to turn me on, Six?"

"Yeah. It working?"

Holden nodded. "Yes, I would say so. Like I said, I was half-convinced you weren't *really* into this."

"Considerate, but you couldn't convince me to do something unless I wanted to do it." Six's brow lifted. "I know you're used to influencing people with your empath shit."

"Wrong." Holden's smile grew wider and sharper. "I don't influence people into fucking me. If I project, I tell them I'm doing it. Most people get off on it. Especially another empath. They're fun to take to bed. I get the sensations of fucking while being fucked, and it's glorious. It's led to many a hands-free orgasm."

Six visibly swallowed. His hands curled into loose fists. "So sleeping with an impenetrable will be boring for you?"

"Don't be silly. Sex is never boring." Holden reached out to slide Six's sweatpants down and took the underwear with them. He expected resistance, but got none. Before his body was ready, he was staring at flawless skin, a six-pack he'd like to eat off of, thick thighs, and the thick length of Six's cock. "You're extremely hard."

"I'm extremely horny."

Holden's breath caught right before he released a slow exhale. He gripped Six's shoulders and guided him backward, totally getting off on the arousal flushing Six's skin and causing pre-come to pearl at the tip of his dick. Holden gently pushed him down onto the futon and knelt between those powerful thighs. He could smell musk, and that made him ache.

Six tensed, every muscle flexing. "I'm nervous."

Holden looked up from the thick column in front of him. That dick should have been halfway down his throat by now, but he kept hesitating. And Six's admission, so calmly stated, held him back even more. He hadn't wanted to bottom for someone this much in a long time, but maybe they'd work their way up to that.

"Are you certain you want to do this with me?"

"Yes."

"Why?"

Six tilted his head back against the wall and rolled his eyes up to the ceiling. "Because I haven't been around someone like you in a long time."

"Someone like what?"

"Someone who speaks their mind, no matter how fucking stupid or annoying what they're saying is, and who isn't afraid . . . to want things besides what the Community wants." Six's fingers dug into the cushion. He was so clearly nervous, but he spoke evenly, and with an intensity that heated Holden to the core. "It turns me on. You turn me on. Even though I think you're a spoiled brat half the time, I still want to fuck you until you come harder than you have with any empath."

"Then let's make it happen, Sixtus."

Holden grinned right before he leaned forward and flicked his tongue at the tip of Six's dick. Six tasted good. Strong. Heady enough for Holden to wrap his fingers around the base of that dick. He wanted to take his time and enjoy the pre-come trickling onto his tongue. He lapped at it, savoring each drop no matter how small, and promised to pace himself. Right now his own erection was throbbing and his gut was coiling even while fluttering with excitement, but he needed to make this last.

With one more lick from base to tip, Holden glanced up at Six. He'd closed his eyes, but his brows were pushed together and his lips were parted. It was a pretty enough picture that Holden caught himself gazing up at this work of art in awe instead of worshiping the dick bobbing wetly in front of his mouth.

"Please don't stop," Six whispered. "Feels so good."

"What does it feel like?" Holden asked, dropping wet kisses on each of Six's muscular thighs. "Describe it."

"It feels like you crawled into my skin and turned me inside out."

"Mmm." Holden nuzzled Six's balls before kissing up the side of his dick again. "If you think that now, I can't wait until you fuck me."

Six's eyes slit open, endless night in a face currently creased with restrained pleasure. "Me either."

Holden rewarded that answer by taking Six so deep in his mouth that his lips stretched wide and pubic hair brushed the tip of his nose.

"Christ, Holden," Six said in a low guttural voice. "Oh my God."

There was nothing to do in response but look up and flash a mischievous smile. Then he started to suck in earnest. He loved it. Loved the strain of his mouth, the ache of his neck, and the feel of those powerful hands bracing the back of his head in an effort to get deeper. Even while almost choking before finding a rhythm to accommodate Six's size, Holden immersed himself in the feeling of his mouth being used and the image of Six's large masculine body hunching over him.

And without the ability to dive into Six's head and experience his side of things, the way Holden had with so many other lovers, all he could do was focus on the taste and smell.

The strength in Six's hands was enough of a turn-on by itself. Pairing it with Six's decadent moans was almost too much for Holden to take. He reached down with one hand to stroke his own erection, needing some relief as his mouth was invaded.

What had started as tentative thrusts elevated into fingers twining tightly in his hair as Six slid in and out of his mouth. He'd widened his thighs and was humping Holden's face with such force that his balls slapped Holden's chin. Six seemed determined to get in as deep as possible, and Holden was happy to open wide and make that happen. Happy to be nothing more than a vessel of pleasure for this poor beautiful man who'd gone untouched for so long.

"I'm gonna come."

It was said like a warning, or a signal for Holden to stop. That wasn't his style. He grabbed the base again and pumped the saliva-covered shaft until hot spurts of semen hit the back of his throat. Six's shocked moans nearly sounded like sobs. Holden relished in the noises as well as the erotic taste bursting over his tongue. Only when he'd swallowed every drop, did he back off.

Six's breath was ripping out of him in loud gasps as he slowly unwound his fingers from Holden's hair. He was locked up and tense, chest heaving. With his brows pushed together and arched, eyelashes damp, and lips parted, he looked like he'd just lost his mind.

Sitting back on his haunches, Holden ignored his own erection and simply feasted on Six's body. On his blown-away expression, curled toes, and gripping fingers. The beauty of his hard tattooed biceps, cut abs, and thick thighs made him exactly the kind of man Holden would have normally taken great pride in undoing. It would have felt like a conquest, and the gloating would have been on another level of obnoxious. But this was different. There was no smugness turning up Holden's mouth or dragging sassy comments out. He just stared at the stoic man whose voice had gone so high and vulnerable as he came, and wanted more. Wanted to get inside his head and figure out what Six was feeling besides the sated ecstasy of just having had an orgasm.

Holden put his hands on Six's knees and slid them up his thighs. Six's eyes slit open so he could gaze at Holden beneath his lashes.

"Do you want to stop?"

Six opened his mouth to respond, but no sound came out. He cleared his throat. "No, but you need to give me a few minutes to get hard again."

Holden didn't try to hide his big smile.

"We can do other things in the meantime."

Six's gaze skimmed him again. "Like what?"

"Are you opposed—"

His phone interrupted, ringing loudly in his pocket. Irritation warmed Holden, but he jerked it out. Ignoring the call was a necessity if he was going to keep this sex train running before Six got skittish and changed his mind, but it was Lia's name flashing on the screen.

"I need to take this," he reluctantly said.

"Do what you need to do."

Holden needed to climb on that dick and ride it like a cowboy once Six was hard again, but that wasn't in the cards right now. He stood up and paced away from the futon, facing the large windows that looked out on the Hudson. The late-evening sun was a beautiful deep gold reflecting off the water, which should have been an enchanting view, but his gut was clenching in anticipation for whatever Lia would say to him now.

"Holden," she said, breathless. "Elijah's gone."

"What—" Holden glanced at Six, who was keenly watching him. "What do you mean—gone?"

"We got in an argument about you, so I walked out, but I felt bad about the way I'd left things, so I returned. I found his door cracked, that apartment ransacked, and no Elijah. He's fucking gone."

CHAPTER SEVEN

The Airbnb apartment Elijah had been staying in wasn't just ransacked—it was destroyed.

Knickknacks were knocked off their shelves and smashed to the floor, chairs were broken, and the mattress had been dragged halfway off the frame. His clothes were everywhere, but that looked like a result of his suitcase having been knocked over and caught in the middle of a scuffle. Even so, the sight of Elijah's clothing trampled and torn up shook Holden. Elijah was tough and mouthy when he needed to be, but could he defend himself against hulking Community cronies? Probably not. And the mental image of his petite frame being dragged out of the apartment made Holden want to vomit.

He knelt on the floor and ran his hand over the broken chair, a ripped T-shirt, and the shards of a smashed porcelain ornament. The impressions washing over him were so strong he had to jerk his hand away. The stink of fear permeated the area, but it was punctuated by the determination of Elijah's attackers, Elijah's rage and then frustration. It was all so strong that Holden was temporarily transported from this reality and into another one—where the struggle played out dimly before his eyes.

"Holden?"

Snapping out of his daze of visualizing, Holden looked up at Lia. She was stricken. Big eyes bloodshot and mouth tight at the sides. She was as shaken as him, maybe more so, but she held herself together with grim determination, refusing to show her fear and worry to someone she didn't fully trust. Someone with the last name Payne.

"They didn't ransack the place," he said hoarsely. "Nothing is taken. They only came for him, and he fought back. I can feel how annoyed they were that this easy mark, a short gay kid who's barely a hundred and thirty pounds, was causing them so much trouble. I'm sure they didn't expect him to be such a wildcat."

"I'm sure they didn't. And I bet he kicked at least one of them in the balls."

Lia sank to the floor beside Holden and stared down at one of Elijah's Dreadnought tank tops. For just a minute, it looked like she would shatter. Her eyes grew moist and her lower lip trembled. Holden knew that if she cracked, he would too. His stomach had been roiling since he'd fled Six's apartment, and his self-control was frayed. Elijah had been close to him for as long as Elijah had been in the Comm, and the idea of someone hurting him . . .

"Fuck. If you cry, I'm going to cry," he croaked.

Lia blinked and ripped a hand across her face. "Who's crying?"

"No one. Never mind." Holden sniffed and staggered to his feet. The abrupt movement left him lightheaded. "Why would anyone do this?"

"It's not anyone," she said harshly. "It's the Community. And you know."

His stomach soured. He wanted to deny it with every fiber of his being, but how could he? It had been Comm thugs trying to get to Elijah for months. Trying to coax him to go with them, and then stalking him after he said no. Maybe that was even what had happened now. They'd once again tried to talk him into compliance, he'd refused, and their orders had been to drag him along regardless of his consent.

"Are you really going to pretend this isn't related to the Comm?" Lia asked, voice rising. "You can't be that far in denial, Holden. You knew they were following him."

"*I know*," he snapped. "I just . . . Listen, I believe there may be a dark element inside the Community, but I'm more inclined to think this is all connected to covering up the situation with Beck than some other wild conspiracy."

"'Wild conspiracy,'" she repeated. "They dragged Elijah out of his apartment *by force*, and you still think what I said is unlikely? For fuck's sake, Holden. What will it take to convince you that all of this—the CW, the board, the rules to keep us quiet and compliant, the money—it's all designed to have an army of ignorant, loyal psychics, so you can all be used for whatever the hell they want to use you for. And it helps if they can cherry-pick the stronger of you to be their super soldiers and plants."

"Because that sounds absolutely batshit," he shouted. "And tell me what all of that would have to do with Elijah? He's a precog, but he's not a powerful one. He knows the details of what went down with Beck, but so does Chase. Why would they need Elijah?"

"You just answered your own question." Lia stood with a groan, wincing and favoring her knee. "Chase knew what Beck was up to, and he told Elijah everything at the end. Now they're both gone. And like you said, the board, your father included, is *very* invested in covering that situation up."

Holden's heart seized, and his gut clenched again. "You can't mean . . . You don't think they'd . . . that someone would kill them, do you?"

"I don't know. Someone killed Theo. Jericho." Lia closed her eyes briefly. She took a deep breath. "I think Chase is too powerful an asset for them to get rid of, but I have no idea what they'll do to Elijah. Maybe they'll subject them both to realignment up at the Farm and put them on display as good little Comm groupies to win back some sense of calm and trust. Or maybe they'll—"

His mother's voice filled Holden's head. The empty platitudes, the automatic defense of the Community and Holden's father, and the shrill panic in her voice when he'd mentioned the investigation. How she'd sounded like a different person. Or worse—a vessel for Community propaganda.

"Maybe they'll hold them at the Farm and brainwash them both," Holden said softly. "Erase what happened, erase their doubts and what they know, and then turn them loose again to show that all of these rumors and gossip are untrue. That everything is fine and there was never a crack in the Community's wall of trust."

Lia said nothing, but she was nodding slowly.

"What I don't understand is how they found him," Holden said. "He got this place just a week or so ago. Unless he used his real social media to connect to the website and book the room, I don't understand how they tracked him when he's been laying low. They haven't had the opportunity to follow him."

Lia strode to the windows and peered through the curtains. "Are you sure *you* weren't followed?"

"Me? No, I—" Holden shut his mouth with an audible click. The sick feeling returned. "Six. Six has been following me."

Lia stilled but didn't look back at him. "You've seen him?"

"No, but he told me. He . . ." Holden braced a hand against the wall. "He'd previously made me aware of the goons tailing Elijah. This morning, I ran into him after I left here. He'd admitted to following me around sometimes but said it was to make sure no one else was. Claimed he didn't like his assignment being . . . infringed upon by Community thugs."

"Do you believe him?"

There should have been doubt in Holden's heart now that he was sitting in the ruins of Elijah's brief hideaway, but there wasn't. He couldn't get inside of Six's head and verify his words, or feel any vibes that would have given away whether he was lying or not, but Holden believed him. Even though he couldn't explain why.

"Yes. I do."

Surprisingly, Lia didn't scorn him for the statement. She turned and pressed her back to the window, her face drawn with exhaustion. "Then we need to figure out how they found him. Six would have noticed if he was being followed. He's good."

"How could you possibly know that?"

"Because I've heard of him and what he's capable of."

"What's that?" Holden asked, bewildered. "He's practically a void."

"There's that toxic Community attitude that turned your girl Beck into a monster," Lia scoffed. "Listen, Holden, you need to get it out of your head that not having abilities makes a person *just* anything. They're not lesser. Six definitely isn't. If Chase is the superhuman version of a psychic, Six is one minus the psychic talent. Since he was a kid, they taught him to be formidable enough to protect the Community. He may not have the mental gifts, but be sure that boy can take on every single person in the Comm when it comes to hand-to-hand fighting. He has a different kind of strength."

That Holden believed. He'd felt it in that body when it had been so close to his own. And he'd felt it in those hands as they'd gripped the back of his head.

He ran a hand through his hair and released a ragged sigh. "If it's not Six, then we have no idea how they tracked me *or* you," he said. "And we don't know where to start. So, if you don't have any other ideas, I think it's about damn time I confront my father."

Lia's eyes went so wide the whites around her pupils were visible. "You've lost your fucking mind."

"No. I haven't. But this isn't a game, Lia. We're not the psychic version of Veronica Mars sleuthing around for clues. Real people are missing. Our *friends* are missing. We need to—"

"First off? Don't talk down to me, Holden. Your dumb ass didn't even have a clue about anything being wrong in the Community until it was explicitly spelled out for you."

Holden nearly swallowed his own tongue. "Sorry. I'm just upset."

"Understandable, but getting on my bad side will do nothing but get my foot up your ass." She crossed her arms over her chest and stared him down like she was seriously considering doing just that. "I'm gonna tell you right now that talking to your father about this is a bad plan. If he knows that me and Elijah are affiliated with Ex-Comm, that Six is—"

"I wouldn't say that. I'll just—" Holden gestured vaguely, searching for a way to demand an explanation without giving too much away. "I'll just say what I've witnessed at the club. That I've seen people following Elijah and now he's missing. I don't have to bring up anything else at all."

"And when he denies being involved?" she challenged. "Or worse—when he decides to confess that he *is* involved and tries to reel you into his plot? What will you do then?"

"That's not going to happen."

"How do you know? Because you don't think your father is the sociopathic monster that I know him to be?"

Holden bristled. "I know my father only cares about his own agenda and his goals. And I know he can be cold. I just don't think the entire Community is a manifestation of that. And I refuse to believe that's why it was created."

For some reason it was those words that softened Lia. "Fine. Feel him out. I'll trust you to not fuck it up."

"Well, thank you for that vote of confidence," he said drolly. "Any advice?"

"Yeah—keep your cool. Your father may be *basically a void*, but that doesn't mean there aren't other Evolution employees under his thumb. Keep your shields up, Holden. And keep your fucking cool. Don't show your hand."

"I won't. If there's anything I can do, it's be phony. I learned the art of white knuckling through a false smile from the woman who married my awful father."

For many people, Richard Payne *was* the Community. Maybe not the only founder, but certainly the most prominent one. He was the face everyone saw at Community Watch, and the one who appeared to play bad cop if someone broke a rule or needed to be put into line. Everyone knew him. The other founders—Kyger and Hale—were more of an enigma. And people preferred a recognizable face to a cipher.

What most people didn't understand was that Richard Payne inserted himself into so many situations because he was a control freak, not a worried Community dad. And he was so prominent at the CW because he lived on the top floor of the building, which was why Holden had keys to the place. Once upon a time, it had been his home as well. He'd come home from his private school with the psychic teachers and administration on the Upper East Side, and run around the building as his mother did her rounds on each floor. While she'd worked to meet new intakes and speak with the staff, Holden had tried to help but mostly observed or got under her feet. Even so, he'd liked to spend time with his mother, and he'd loved seeing the new psychics.

Looking back, Holden could identify how privileged he was. How much of a bubble he'd lived in. How ridiculous it had been for this filthy-rich child to poke his head in the rooms of psychics who'd been rescued from homeless shelters and psych wards. People who'd been thrown away by people who should have loved them. That lack of awareness, even years later, was mortifying.

He entered the high-rise through a back door and took the elevator up, bypassing other people and more populated floors. Even on Christmas, there was activity at the CW. There was an annual holiday party for fledgling Comm members with no family of their own, a gift exchange, and a Christmas movie marathon. As a young person, Holden had taken part in many of these activities and had volunteered his time to help host them. It was why he couldn't believe the Community, and specifically the CW, had been created solely for evil.

But then again, Lia had a point. It wasn't the Paynes or the Kygers or the Hales who ran these events, or even who'd come up with them. They were figureheads in charge of bigger issues and had long since left other folks in charge of the programs on the ground. In the past, that distance had bothered Holden. Now, he wondered if they'd started participating less because altruism and philanthropy had never been their true goal.

And, fuck, now he was getting paranoid and buying into Lia's theories. He barely knew Kyger or Hale, but he'd begun dragging them into it all.

Holden left the elevator while repeating a mantra to forget the conspiracy. He wouldn't let it color his interactions with his father. Not yet, anyway. If he didn't go in with a clear head, the conversation would end in disaster. That much was certain.

He told himself that again while working up the courage to actually knock, but all of his resolve evaporated once it swung open before he could raise his hand.

The man who appeared in the doorway was not his father, but he was definitely familiar. He had a tattoo on his face of a thin black band that went over the bridge of his nose and around his bright-green cat eyes. It was the man from Holden's and Elijah's dreams.

Holden's mouth fell open, but no sound came out. Words failed him, and coherent thought fled. He could do nothing but stand and stare at the person only a few inches away. A person he'd never met in person, but who emitted the type of vibes that curdled Holden's stomach and sent invisible insects skittering over his skin. It was like being face-to-face with a personification of evil.

"Holden," the man said simply.

"I—" His tongue was too thick and was preventing him from forming words. His mouth too dry and his heart was beating too fast. "Who are you? Where's my father?"

"Your father is in the kitchen where I left him."

Holden forced a jerky nod, but he didn't move. Not into the apartment or out of the man's way. He tried to take in other things about the man with the cat eyes—how he was thin and lanky with tattooed symbols on each finger, had a shaved head and a down-curved mouth. How every other feature was utterly unremarkable except those eyes and the tattoo.

What was it about him that made Holden want to sprint in the opposite direction? That jumpstarted the electric shocks of impending doom and danger?

Knowing better but unable to stop himself, Holden reached out with his gift. He'd expected a door to slam shut on the tentatively seeking tendrils, but instead he received vibes so strong they were undeniably being projected by the other man. A vague sense of amusement and the colder darker fingers of caution. But was the man cautioning himself to be careful around Holden . . . or was he warning Holden to back off? There was no way to tell, so Holden shut off the connection and slammed down his own mental shields.

"Who are you?" he asked after another beat. "I thought I'd met everyone affiliated with the Community."

"Most people don't know me. My name is Jasper. My primary position places me at the Farm."

The admission made it certain that Chase was at the Farm. And Holden knew without a shadow of a doubt that this man, Jasper, was involved in his brother's realignment or incarceration—whatever it was they were doing to Chase.

"Then what are you doing here?"

"Visiting the man in charge." Jasper's smile was sharp and vacant. "We're working on a special project, and he likes his updates in person."

Special project. Was that project about Chase? Or Elijah?

A stone formed in the pit of Holden's stomach.

"You had me at 'special project,'" he said with a crooked grin. "Care to satisfy my curiosity?"

Jasper cocked his head. "I'd recommend asking your father about that. Now if you'll excuse me . . ."

He slipped past Holden in the doorway to make his way to the elevator. They didn't touch, but an arctic wind seemed to come off the man, and it sent a shudder sweeping through Holden's body.

Shaking himself, he entered the apartment and shut the door behind him. As always, the Payne penthouse looked like an untouched showroom in a furniture store. Beautiful, elegantly styled, but uninhabitable. Like a museum. Richard was in the kitchen preparing a meal, but everything was still unnaturally orderly. Not a stray towel out of place or a water stain on any of the stainless-steel appliances.

"What's going on?"

Richard didn't look up. "You've decided against announcing your visits, I see."

"I didn't realize that I needed to make an appointment."

"It would be wise given I'm typically not here." Richard stopped slicing a perfectly sliced onion and brushed his hands on a paper towel. "I'm only here because I had a meeting."

"With Jasper," Holden said.

"Yes. With Jasper." Richard put his hand on the chopping knife and left it there as he scrutinized him. "What can I do for you, Holden?"

It was a straightforward question but asked in such a tone of indifference, as if they were two strangers meeting for the first time in a doctor's office, that a flip switched inside of Holden. "You can start by telling me why my mother is a zombie, where you've put my brother, and why you have Community henchmen following my friends."

"'Your friends,'" Richard repeated. "Meaning Elijah Estrella?"

"Yes. Elijah Estrella. The drummer for the Dreadnoughts, part-time bartender at Evolution, sometime lover of Chase, and my goddamn friend."

Richard moved his hand away from the knife. "What do you gain by being friends with an individual like Elijah?"

An incredulous laugh burst out of Holden's mouth. "'Gain'? He's my *friend*. I don't hope to gain anything. And I'm not sleeping with him so you can hold off on that accusation, because I know it's coming."

"It wouldn't have been an accusation. In this case, it's the only thing that makes sense. The only commonality the two of you have is that you're in the Community and you're gay." Richard pushed the chopping board away and walked around the counter. Everything about him was precise and controlled. Inhuman. "What else could you possibly want with him, Holden?"

"I already told you we're friends. I could not care less about his net worth or the extent of his psychic abilities. Those things don't mean anything to me. I'm not like that." The unspoken *I'm not like you* hung in the air. They both knew he was thinking it. "What I'm attempting to grasp is, if you think Elijah is a waste of time and a useless addition to our community, why is he being followed?"

Impatience gathered on Richard's brow, the clouds of the brewing storm of his unleashed temper. It was never shouting with him. Richard Payne's anger came like a blizzard that blanketed the person on the receiving end of his disapproval. Nothing but cold disgust and very quiet rage.

"He's being monitored because he knows more than he admitted about the situation with Beck. And lying puts him in breach of Community rules as well as labeled a suspect."

"Suspected of doing *what*? Keeping his mouth shut? Trying to stay out of it?"

"Yes. If he had even an inkling that something was going on, he should have reported it. Instead, he followed your brother's example and hid things from us. And at the moment, it's unclear what else they may be hiding."

Holden's hand slammed down on the counter before he could rein it in. "Are you really going to pursue this, Father? This ridiculous witch hunt to find a scapegoat for *your* fuckup? Because it was *you* who placed Beck here. *You* also missed the fact that she was a goddamn vampire because you were too worried about getting someone to spy on me." He laughed, a harsh, ugly sound that echoed in the large kitchen. "What I can't work out is why you sent *her*. Was it because she was sleeping with you and you knew she'd report accurately due to her loyalty, or was it because you thought she was basically a void, and had no other use for her beyond sex? That seems more your speed."

Unexpectedly, Richard laughed. A low, long chuckle that brightened his face and gave some life to the still apartment.

"Holden, you really are fixated on how I view people without significant talent, aren't you?"

"Yes. I am," he said directly. "I used to feel similarly until I realized that social hierarchy does nothing more than alienate members of the community and create people like Beck."

"That's where you're wrong, son. Our social structure didn't create Beck. Greed did. And jealousy. She knew how we valued her gift, and she knew why power is so key to the Community thriving."

"I thought you created the Community to help people like Elijah," Holden said. "And Chase."

"Initially we did, but change doesn't stop there. We have to be proactive, Holden. And to be proactive we have to be on the inside."

"The inside . . ."

"Yes. And we can only infiltrate the circles that influence this country by amassing psychics with real power. Psychics like the men and women Beck targeted, like your brother, and like the Black family." There was a beat of silence where Richard leaned forward, brows lowered, and stared into Holden's eyes as if he was trying to see where his interests lay, whether Holden was understanding this new mission statement, and likely wondering whether Holden would help. *Are you an ally or a weak link?* "For us to succeed, we need power and we need loyalty. And those who aren't loyal, who aren't honest and committed, serve as an Achilles' heel to the entire organization. Their choices are to realign or to be gone."

CHAPTER EIGHT

A week went by with no sign of Elijah.

His phone stopped ringing and went straight to voice mail, and the place he'd been renting on Airbnb remained in a state of chaos. No one had returned to tidy it, so Holden did when he checked in for the fifteenth time since Christmas.

He folded each small article of clothing neatly and packed them away in Elijah's purple suitcase, and then went about the task of sweeping up the broken knickknacks. Never having stayed in an Airbnb, Holden wasn't sure how the damage should be reported. He didn't even know who owned the apartment or how to get in touch with them. Surely there was a way to find the information online.

Holden finished cleaning and looked around the small apartment. There were times like these when he wished that his ability was stronger. That he could do something beyond pick up vibrations of fear and rage and frustration as he swept away the evidence of the struggle. A postcog could hone in on those sensations and conjure an actual vision of the event. They'd be able to see who took Elijah. They'd know if he was okay.

Stomach tightening, Holden sank down to the couch and pulled out his phone. He searched the building's address on Airbnb and quickly found the corresponding ad. The weekly price was three hundred dollars—dirt cheap for the area—and it was being sublet by a woman named Kiara Arredondo. She described the space as artsy and fun, perfect for a traveling student or a tourist wanting to be in the heart of Manhattan in an apartment that was also . . . near Community Watch. There was a note stating "soon-to-be C members get a discounted rate! Message for details."

Holden reread the two lines several times before practically tossing his phone down on the coffee table.

She was a psychic. Elijah had sublet the room from a member of the fucking Community.

How could he have been so stupid?

"Goddamn it, Elijah."

The apartment went from being a shattered portrait of whimsy and charm to . . . something else. A setup. A trap. Another honeypot used to lure in fresh new psys who'd somehow heard of the Community and were looking to put down roots in the city. How many places like this were there dotted around the city? The East Coast? Maybe even in the country? Just how far were his father, and the other board members, going to ensure they got first pick of newly minted Comm members with powers that would help them get a leg up in their bigger-picture plans?

Holden hurried out of the apartment and jogged down the stairs of the building. There was a large chance he was jumping the gun. After all, Kiara could just be like him—someone who was loyal to the Community and who was trying to give back by helping less fortunate psychics who were looking to find a safe space where they could be open. Where they could belong. It could be altruism. Not part of a plot.

After bursting into the frigid December air, Holden took deep gulping breaths that fogged up in front of him. The cold was abrupt after the ramped-up heat inside the building, but it helped to push aside his frantic thoughts and attempts to rationalize this growing conspiracy theory. Because even if that apartment was marketed to psys solely to provide room and board, it didn't change that Elijah had disappeared from there, which was too much of a coincidence to be one at all.

Holden sucked in another breath and shot Lia a text message: *call me when you can. i think i know how they found Elijah.*

He waited a few minutes, standing in the middle of the sidewalk as a steady flow of harried New Yorkers rushed by in their wool coats and scarves, but she didn't respond. The desire to share this information with someone else, to have a witness, consumed Holden to the point where his finger hovered over Six's number. He brushed the screen with his thumb before slipping the phone back into his pocket.

Why had that even presented itself as an option? They'd fucked around once. That didn't make them confidantes. It didn't make them anything. In the past week, they'd barely spoken—although that could have had more to do with Holden's recent tendency to avoid the club than anything else. It was difficult to patrol the floors of Evolution and watch scores of intoxicated youths lose themselves in music and each other, while the ghosts of Holden's past faded away. With each successful party and each night they reached capacity, Holden felt guilt instead of pleasure. The club might have been in an upswing from the depressed state of the past couple of months, but the people who'd made it special were all gone—the Dreadnoughts, the band that had initially been such a big draw in the early days. They were dead, or vanished, and he was still there upping cover charges and drink prices. Being a capitalist instead of a friend. Getting richer instead of mourning.

Was it normal to feel this awful about having survived?

There was no answer in his head or his heart, so he shelved the question and caught a taxi to the club.

The New Year's Eve party was in full swing when Holden entered Evolution. There was a line down the block, and Six was manning the door with a stone face and eyes as cold as the strengthening wind. He glanced at Holden once as he brushed by, but they didn't speak. At this point, it wasn't a surprise. Maybe he was done being cordial now that he'd gotten his dick sucked. Or maybe he'd learned of Elijah's disappearance and was keeping his distance so as not to get involved.

Unless he already was involved, which was why he was keeping his distance.

There would come a point when paranoia ate Holden inside out. He knew it, but he didn't know what to do about it.

"We're already at capacity," Kamryn said after Holden stopped at the bar to grab a bottle for his planned night of isolation in the office. "It's not even ten o'clock, H. That's fucking nuts."

"Yes. We're doing very well lately."

Kamryn curled her lips in an exceptionally dramatic stank face. "You seem really excited about it."

He flashed a faint smile. "It's been a long year. You could say I'm feeling a little hesitant about the new one."

"Why? This is the perfect time to hope for a change in the tides or whatever the hell optimistic assholes say."

This time, he outright laughed. Leave it to Kamryn to be a bright spot in his otherwise dismal day. Week. Month.

"Maybe there will be a change for the better. It would be hard for next year to be as catastrophically awful as this year."

"Yeah, I mean, ideally there will be no kidnappings or murders."

"Right." Holden's smile faded. He grabbed the neck of a bottle of bourbon and skirted the bar again. "Exactly."

"Sorry. Was that tactless?"

"No. It was honest." He held up his prize while nodding toward the spiral staircase. "I'll be in my office if you need me. Six has everything in hand down here."

"He's had everything in hand all week, H. You should think about giving the guy a holiday bonus."

"Maybe," he agreed.

Or maybe his father had already given Six one.

Holden hurried upstairs and was thankful that people were no longer expecting his attention. In the past, he'd played the part of host instead of owner, moving from customer to customer to gauge the level of their enjoyment, whether drinks were coming out fast enough, and to make small talk with the regular psy folk. Now things were different. He didn't want those close connections with people who might be at the club for purposes other than drinking, or were potentially being targeted by the Community for unknown purposes. The more distance between Holden and the people around him, the better. Except for Six.

Being close to Six would be advantageous on so many levels—learning what Richard Payne truly wanted him to do at Evolution, whether Six had seen Chase or Holden's mother at the Farm, or if the moment they'd shared had ruined any hope of Holden ever getting answers to those questions. After all, Six had claimed he'd been intrigued by Holden. That there was something about him that had drawn Six's attention from the beginning. Had all of that been bullshit? Holden wasn't used to being played. Especially by his own mark.

With the bottle of bourbon open and the amber liquid filling a glass that likely had foregone washing for a couple of days, Holden slumped in his chair and stared at the computer monitor. It was the perfect way to check on the party without putting himself in the middle of the chaos of humanity, but he couldn't focus on the dance floor or the bar. His eyes flit from camera to camera, hoping against hope that he'd catch a glimpse of Elijah. That all of this had been a nightmare, and the young precog had been safe all along. Or maybe that he'd faked an abduction to get the Community off his back. It was an absurd theory, but Holden was desperate.

If this was real life, it meant that the Community wasn't above kidnapping and punishing psys who didn't fit their mold of a loyal and committed Comm member. It meant they weren't above brainwashing. That they didn't actually see any of them as real people with free will. Which made it even more likely that Lia was right, and that his father might have become a monster over time. Maybe even the rest of the board.

It would also mean that Holden wasn't much better than his brainwashed mother if he was completely frozen with fear at the idea of contacting local law enforcement and getting voids involved. If he knew anything about his father, and the Community, it was that involving outsiders was a sign of betrayal. That was how all of this mess had started. According to his father, he'd "allowed" the police to get involved with the disappearances. From that point on, he'd been saddled with a babysitter. Who knew what would happen this time?

He tossed back a drink, let it burn down his throat, and slid his gaze to the mammoth bulletin board dominating most of the opposite wall. A year ago, Elijah had insisted on decorating the office. He'd said it was gloomy and depressing and that it needed some life. What better way to put some life into a space than by filling it with pictures of himself?

The bulletin board was covered by a collage of photographs—fifty percent Elijah with his cheeky grin, booty shorts, and various outrageously flashy shirts, and several more with him and Chase or the Dreadnoughts. All at the club, back before the vanishings and the deaths and the mysteries. Back when Evolution had simply been a happy place for queer psys who had been demeaned or dismissed by the rest of the Community. Because even in an organization full of freaks, they were still the fucking outcasts.

He swallowed his bitterness and chased it with another swig of bourbon. It didn't help. The discontent and suspicion, the fear and rage, were roiling together deep inside of him and feeding the part of him that knew there was something to Lia's claims.

Holden shoved back his chair and walked over to the bulletin board. He touched the pictures of people who had once been his friends, before letting his fingers hover over a snapshot of Chase at Coney Island. It was an old Polaroid and faded with time, but the moment was engraved in his mind. It had been one of the first trips they'd gone on as a "family," shortly after Chase had been released from the Farm. He'd been so haunted as a child. Big gray eyes wide and guarded as he kept his smiles and words scant. He'd kept so much to himself that Holden had no idea how long Chase had known about the Black family—about the mother who'd fled the Community and the twin brothers who'd been stowed away down in Texas.

Had he known all along, or had he learned just before contacting Nate?

Nate . . .

Out of everyone in the Community, and the Ex-Comm or whatever Lia had called it, it had been Nate and his void boyfriend who'd backed Beck into a corner. Although Nate had claimed his empath abilities were weak, he was the one who'd figured everything out and put a stop to it all. He hadn't hesitated to investigate his brother's death, and he hadn't been cowed by any of them.

Before Holden could rethink the decision, he had his phone out and he was dialing Nate's number. There was a pause before it rang, and he feared the number had been disconnected and changed, but it rang. It rang four times before voice mail picked up.

"Nate," he said haltingly. "It's Holden. Look—I kept my word and left your name out of it, but . . . Chase is gone. He's been missing for a while, and I don't know what to do—"

The door to the office burst open. Holden stiffened, still facing the bulletin board, and hung up without finishing the sentence. From the lack of impressions coming off the person who'd stepped into the room, he knew it was Six.

"Shouldn't you be down there monitoring the door and making sure only Community folks get in?"

"That's a wash," Six said. "It's too crowded. The line would get hostile."

"And you care about them getting hostile?"

"No. But I figured you wouldn't want me pissing off your regulars. Even the voids."

"Heh. You're pretty intuitive for an impenetrable."

Six joined him next to the bulletin board. He slid his hands into the pockets of the black-and-gray camo cargo pants he wore way too often. "You're a bigoted motherfucker."

Holden couldn't have glared more incredulously had Six accused him of being a conservative. "Excuse me?"

"You're a bigot."

Holden ground his teeth together. "How am I a bigot?"

"You don't like non-psychics. You think we're lesser than you."

"Okay, no." Holden fully faced him. "First—*you're* a psychic. Just because your brain is a giant EMP wave for psychic abilities doesn't mean you're a void. Your gift is just more passive than mine."

"You're the first person to ever put it that way," Six said, raising an eyebrow. "Shocking."

"Yes, it's *shocking* that I have half a brain." Holden narrowed his eyes. "Second—I don't dislike voids. I just have little patience for them."

"You think you're smarter than them. Hell, you think you're smarter than me, and that is definitely a product of your delusions of grandeur. Me being an impenetrable doesn't mean I don't have common sense, Holden. And you implying it does just makes you a giant douche bag."

"Are you less likely to let me give you another blowie if I act like a douche bag?"

Six's mouth twitched. He ran his tongue over his teeth as if to prevent himself from flashing even an eighth of a smile. "Don't say 'blowie.'"

"Fine, but the question still stands."

"Heh." Six went back to eyeballing the photographs. "We could fuck around again. If I get to touch you next time."

There should have been an explosion of triumph in Holden's chest, but he felt nothing. Just a distant satisfaction that Six still wanted him, which collided with his original plan to use sex to get information. Although he had no idea how likely it was that a guy who merely said, *We could fuck around again*, would form enough of an emotional attachment to spill any of the beans.

"Er, yes, there would not be complaining from me there."

Six slowly nodded. "Cool."

"Yeah. Cool."

When Holden didn't say anything more, Six looked at him sidelong. "What's with you?"

"Nothing."

"After all that game you spit on Christmas, all you've got is *cool*? Bullshit."

"That was before," Holden said.

"Before what?" Six's brows drew together when his question earned him no answer. "Did something happen?"

"Come on, Six. You know it did."

Six's lips curled down. He crossed his arms over his chest, shoulders back. "I was put here to keep you out of trouble and make sure the club is keeping the psychics happy. That's it. Anything else that goes on has nothing to do with me, Holden. I can tell you that right now."

Holden cycled through responses, and wondered why he was on the brink of blurting out the truth. There was something about Six, his straightforward demeanor and bottomless dark eyes, that made Holden feel like their conversations were their own. Not repeated for anyone else. Not fodder for another plan. When he searched Six's face, he found absolutely no indication that this was a game or part of a job. Even without the ability to reach out with his empathy and verify these suspicions, Holden trusted his instincts.

He trusted Six.

Maybe he didn't have to fuck the man to get some answers.

"Do you want to go somewhere and talk?"

"When? I don't want to leave the—"

This time it was Holden flashing a slight smile. "I'm not suggesting you leave your post, but don't think I'm not endeared by your dedication. I meant later. We could do a 4 a.m. breakfast?"

"Fine. But I like my pancakes homemade."

Was this Six's way of saying he wanted to fuck and eat breakfast in bed? Judging by the way he was looking Holden up and down, it sure seemed like it.

CHAPTER NINE

Four o'clock in the morning in Midtown Manhattan was magical whether or not you had psychic powers.

With Holden worn out and exhausted, his mental shield was down by default. Even in the wee hours, a walk from Evolution, now shuttered and darkened, to Ninth Avenue to catch a cab, led to a million impressions slamming into him from all sides. He felt the horny drunk folks stumbling home, agitated third-shift employees, the slinky cold malice of someone dangerous scheming somewhere in the shadows, and a million other emotions ranging from resentment to heartbreak to unquenched excitement.

By the time they slid into the back of a cab heading to Holden's apartment, he was wound tight and on the edge of the seat.

Was this what Nate felt like all the time? There was no way to know, but the question reminded Holden that Nate had never returned his call. Maybe he wouldn't, and he'd ignore the message. Maybe he'd removed himself completely from the mess of the Community now that he was safely tucked away with his lover. But Chase was Nate's brother too, and if he'd gone through so much to draw Nate across the country to help investigate Theo's murder, could he really ignore his remaining bloodline?

A cool dry hand slid over Holden's, jerking him out of the cloud of his thought. Ignoring the first instinct to pull away, he gave Six a startled look.

"What—"

The flood of impressions ceased as though someone had sheared off the connections. With them went the clatter of his thoughts. Astonishment washed over Holden.

"How did you do that?"

Six arched an eyebrow, looking like an asshole even though he'd just saved the last remnants of Holden's sanity. "Do what?"

"Everything stopped." Holden nodded at the window. "All of the impressions that have been battering my skull for the past few hours. As soon as you touched me, it stopped."

"How do you know it's me?"

Holden moved his hand from beneath Six's and instantly winced as the onslaught rammed into him. Six grabbed his hand again, and it all faded away. He couldn't feel Six's emotions, but Holden could feel the power of the other man's gift. It was like a blizzard whiting out all the noise and bringing the world to a standstill.

"That's incredible," he said slowly. "It almost feels like you knocked out my third eye, but I'm not . . . alarmed by it. I just feel calm."

"I assume that's a good thing?"

"Yes." Holden exhaled and let his shoulders relax. "It is definitely a good thing."

Six nodded, that glittering onyx gaze burning into the side of Holden's face. "So I guess I should keep touching you, then."

Another unlikely laugh burst out of Holden's mouth. "Jesus, that's the second time you've flirted with me tonight. Are you drunk?"

"No. Just horny."

"One taste and you can't get enough?" Holden asked, dropping his voice lower so the poor cabbie wouldn't hear. "I like it when a man is needy."

"I don't know about needy, but I can't get that blowjob out of my mind," Six said with the exact volume you'd use while speaking over loud music in a club.

"Hush."

"Why?"

"Because the cab driver will hear you."

Six glanced through the Plexiglas divider. "So?"

"So . . . well, maybe he doesn't want to hear us talking about sucking dicks."

"Why would I care?"

Holden snorted. "Never mind. You can go back to flirting with me now."

"I will, but all of the fun shit can wait until after you talk to me about whatever you wanted to talk to me about."

"Ah. Right." The amusement faded. "I may not be up for it after that conversation."

Six nodded and kept running his thumb over Holden's hand. "That bad?"

"Yes," Holden said, looking out the window again. "It's that bad."

They were quiet the rest of the way to his apartment in Chelsea—a holdover from the days when it had been the gayest neighborhood in Manhattan. It wasn't ideal to bring someone he didn't fully trust to his one safe space, but always being on Six's turf didn't feel like the best course of action either. Although, with Six's shield expanding and encompassing them both, the concerns about Six's allegiances had temporarily faded away. For the first time in Holden's life, he could not help but think voids were lucky if their heads were always this quiet. How much more functional would he have been as a youth if his mind hadn't always been so cluttered? What would have gone differently if only he hadn't grown up tailoring his behavior to the feelings—feelings he experienced as though they were his own—of the people around him.

Would he have been more autonomous? Less dependent on approval? Less pleasure seeking? Less attention seeking?

Would he have learned to be satisfied with himself instead of always trying to shift the energy around him?

He didn't know, but he did enjoy this quiet.

Without speaking, Holden led Six into his fourth-floor walk-up with their hands still linked. Six's fingers were damp when Holden shut the door, and they were left in the darkness of the entryway, a sliver of moon tracing up the narrow hallway and the glint of their eyes in the shadows of the door.

It was time to stop clutching Six like a lifeline and accept the return of rushing thoughts, fear, and worry into his life, but Holden couldn't bring himself to do it. With the silence in his head and in the apartment, Holden could hear Six's quickening breath and the clicking sound of him swallowing.

Six was nervous. Holden couldn't sense it, but he could tell. And that realization set his own heart racing. How could a simple touch make this embodiment of masculinity nervous? They'd only held hands, and already Six was on edge.

Holden pushed Six against the wall. With their hands still linked, he pinned them over Six's head and pressed their bodies together so tight he could feel everything. The hard lines and muscle, a faint waver of resistance falling away in favor of ragged inhales and an erection that dug into Holden's thigh. Without the invisible antenna of his gift picking up signals from everything around them, every touch was intensified in a way Holden had never experienced. He felt anchored to the world. To Six.

After an uncharacteristic hesitation, he brought their lips together. The type of kiss you gave in the shadowy corner of a Sunday school, tentative and secret. He was giving Six an out he didn't take.

Instead of turning his face and breaking the hold on his hands, Six leaned into the kiss with a groan. He sought Holden's lips in the darkness and claimed them with a fierce neediness, sucking Holden's lower lip into his mouth, then licking at it until he could explore the wet warmth inside. There were no practiced tongue strokes—just the hungry exploration of a man who'd gone without intimacy for way too long.

Holden released Six's hands to dig his own fingers into that thick dark hair. It'd loosed from its knot, and now hung around his face wildly. Holden wished he could see it, and Six, without it being held back and controlled.

Their hearts pounded against each other, chests pressed just so in the exact spot to make it possible, and Holden wondered if he would have ever noticed that connection without the shield curtaining this escalating make-out session.

"You feel good," Six said against his mouth.

"Then touch the rest of me."

The command earned instant compliance. One of Six's large hands cupped the back of Holden's neck, while the other slid down between them. Six might have been unpracticed, but he seemed to know what he wanted. He went right for the belt, then the button and zipper, and had Holden's pants sliding halfway off his ass so he could palm it. The hard squeeze caused heat to pool in Holden's gut, and the way Six's fingers dug in so tight they rubbed against Holden's hole nearly weakened his knees. So, he was an ass guy. Holden was willing to bet his virgin handler was also a top.

"Tell me what you've been fantasizing about."

"Fucking you."

"I like that fantasy," Holden breathed, jutting his hips against Six's. "How do you fuck me?"

"What do you mean?"

"What position are we in?"

Six's fingers squeezed tighter, as though the question had jolted him. "You're on your hands and knees. I hold on to your shoulders and pound your ass while you jerk yourself off."

"Mmm." Holden licked Six's lower lip and sighed with pleasure when Six chased him, desperate for more. "Is it rough? Gentle? Slow?"

"I try to go slow, but I can't. Feels too good, and . . . I want it too bad."

"What do you want?" Now it was Holden's breath coming faster. He wondered if Six realized the effect his words were having, or if he thought this exchange of information was a matter of utility—*What do you expect from this?*

"I want to slide in you so deep and fuck you so hard that you stop thinking about the fact that your goddamn empath abilities don't work on me. I won't stop fucking you until you're no longer capable of smirking, of smart comments, and the coherency to keep reaching out with your gift. Because I can feel you trying. Every time."

"I can't help it. Until you shielded me, I didn't realize how automatic it is."

"It's second nature for you," Six agreed. "But when I'm inside you, I want your second nature to be slamming back on my cock."

An anguished moan slipped from Holden, and he attacked Six's mouth with another kiss. This was definitely a man who knew what he wanted even though he'd never had the opportunity to act on those desires. It was a real shame, but Holden was happy to open the door to every sex act Six wanted to try. They might not fully trust each other when it came to the Community, but that could be put aside in the bedroom. This was just about them.

Holden stopped playing with Six's hair and used his hands for more useful purposes—getting Six's pants down. "Do you jerk off while you think about fucking me?"

"Yeah," Six said, his voice scraping out thick and low.

"Do you say my name?"

A shudder went through Six, and it was the most glorious thing Holden had ever felt. The fact that he was capable of making this powerful, unflappable man unravel was everything that was good and right in the world. Maybe the only good and right thing that was left.

"Sometimes."

Holden wrapped his hand around both their dicks and slowly stroked. "Will you today?"

Six's groan penetrated a moment that had previously been so quiet it'd felt like a secret. "Yes."

"God," Holden whispered. "I'm trying to keep this light and fun, but you being blunt and no-bullshit is turning me on."

Six's chest quivered with a low throaty laugh. "I thought it usually pissed you off."

"Oh, it does. You piss me off in general. But I like that you tell me exactly what you want."

"Good." Six stepped away from the wall. "Because I want to have sex with you before someone calls one of us and screws up my chance."

It wasn't said with the certainty of a precog, but there was enough reality in it to ward Holden off this back-and-forth and drag Six toward his bedroom. Once they were inside, and he was guiding Six onto his bed, they both shed their shirts. Within a few seconds of impatiently disrobing, they were naked on the bed and completely wrapped in each other. They should have been on a fast track toward Six losing his V card somewhere in Holden's ass, but they couldn't stop kissing. Six cradled the back of Holden's neck and worshiped his mouth until Holden's dick was throbbing with a need for contact.

Holden went back to stroking them both as he lost himself in Six's searching kisses. He enjoyed the stunning contrast between his usual psychically-infused sexual encounters and one that was enclosed in a protective bubble where there was nothing but physical touch and the taste and smell of another man.

"You ready?"

Six nodded and pulled back just enough for Holden to grab condoms and lubricant from his side table. Six put on the condom with trembling hands, while Holden rolled over to get on his hands and knees. One of those cool dry hands slid over his ass and up along his spine before repeating in a firm caress.

"Lube will let you slide in easier."

"I know. I'm not completely oblivious."

Smiling, Holden cradled his head in his arms. "Well, if all you've watched is porn . . . they don't always show the prep."

The click of the bottle uncapping was followed by a low hiss of breath. Holden craned his neck just in time to see Six slowly pumping his dick to smooth the lubricant over the thick length. He'd hunched forward with all that hair curtaining his face, although it was still possible to see his parted lips. His arousal was undeniable, but Holden forced himself to zero in on other things—the tightness in those shoulders, the harsh breathing, and hands that wouldn't steady no matter what Six did.

"Hey," Holden said quietly. "I know this is weird because you can't feel how badly I want you, but I do. It doesn't mean I trust you or the Community—" Six glanced up with a puckered brow "—but I can separate that enough to enjoy a thorough ride. Even if we're enemies tomorrow, I won't regret this unless you think you will."

Six's tongue swept over his lower lip and he, once again, did one of those quick scans of the room. Searching for a camera or a witness or a sign from God. Whatever reassurance he was seeking must have been found because he flashed one of those brief tight smiles.

"I want this."

"Good." Holden cradled his head in his arms again and dipped his back lower so his ass was at just the right position. "Fuck me."

Usually when Holden bottomed, he used his empathy to dive into the man inside of him so he could experience both sensations—being breached and being enveloped by a tight ass. There were times when he got so lost in the decadent rain of impressions that sex became dreamlike, unreal. Later, he'd have a hard time working out what he'd felt and what the man inside of him had felt, and it wouldn't matter because he'd gotten off.

This time was different.

When Six parted his cheeks and pushed inside, Holden felt the burn of his ass stretching, the mild discomfort of that large dick impaling him, and then the thrill of being completely full. His mouth dropped open, gaping against the satiny sheet below him, but he only released a guttural sound. There was a rawness to this that he'd never experienced before, and it twisted him up inside until he was desperately trying to drag his dripping cock against the mattress.

"Fuck, that's so good," Six whispered. "Feels too good. My God."

"Move," Holden managed. "Give me more."

Six thrusted experimentally, a delicious in-out that had Holden's eyes rolling back. Impatient demands tried to burst from his mouth, but he swallowed them and rocked backward, silently encouraging Six to give him the hard fuck he'd promised. He was rewarded with a moan so loud, he didn't think it could have come from the wall of muscle at his back. Milking Six's cock with his ass proved otherwise. Six moaned again, louder this time, and again ran his palm over Holden's back before returning to his plump ass cheeks.

"You look so good like this."

"I know."

Six brought his palm down in a firm crack over Holden's ass. He only got to enjoy the sting for a single heartbeat before Six rocked his hips for another deep thrust. It lit Holden up from the inside out, washing over him like a glorious shower of pleasure, and intensifying each time he was filled. Holden gave up on pithy comments and coherent thinking, and rode back on Six. He reveled in pleasure that sent starbursts exploding behind his eyelids with every pounding entrance into his ass, and started laughing in delirious ecstasy when Six grabbed his shoulders.

His grip was hard, violent, demanding, and utterly perfect when he used the leverage to yank Holden back onto his dick. There would be bruises later, but right now Holden reveled in the crudest fuck he'd ever had, one that was also turning out to be the most consuming. There was no higher power at work, no metaphysics or magic, just the senses that linked Holden to this world. And to Six. The iron length of a man sliding in and out of his hole, the ball sac slapping against his ass, the burn of his hamstring as he spread his thighs wider for more leverage to slam backward, fingers bruising his skin, and the dampness of the sheet against his face from his sweat and saliva.

"Can I come on you?"

"Jesus, yes."

Six ripped himself from Holden's body and within seconds of him removing the condom, hot jets of semen splattered onto Holden's ass and thighs. He didn't know what was more erotic. The feeling of that sticky fluid all over him or Six's wild cries as he released. And then, as promised, there was a hoarsely uttered, "Holden."

An urgent desire to see Six's face took hold of Holden. He flipped onto his back and jerked himself off while gazing up into those heavy-lidded eyes. Six was still stroking himself slowly, working every drop out of his piece. He looked like a work of art with his long hair damp and messy and the moonlight illuminating his heaving chest.

It didn't take long for Holden to come, but when he did, the world seemed to blur around him as awareness briefly went away. When it returned, Holden was gasping and moaning, and he was completely covered in semen.

"My God. You're incredible, Six. I can't believe those people kept you isolated for so long."

It was a thoughtless statement, but suddenly the quiet that had covered them since the cab ride was gone. The hum of vibrations from the world around them closed in on Holden. Most of them were dim except for a single glow of warmth and pleasure and happiness that was emitting right . . . from Six.

Holden's postorgasm daze vanished. He pushed his elbows against the bed to halfway sit up, but before he could even finish the motion, the shroud returned and all was quiet again. He thought at first that he'd imagined the connection. One look at Six proved otherwise. He'd sat back on his haunches, still panting, and was gazing at Holden with open astonishment.

"Holy shit," Holden whispered. "I felt you. I fucking felt you."

"I felt you too," Six said hoarsely.

"What does it mean?"

"I don't know, but I have to tell you something."

Holden did sit up this time. "Tell me."

Six bowed his head, took one last long, deep breath, and then glanced up again. "I'm not Community."

Holden's brows snapped together. "Then what are you?"

"I'm Ex-Comm."

CHAPTER TEN

The heat of their bodies drained away, and goose bumps spread over Holden's skin. He blinked up at Six without speaking, waiting for this to be the joke of an awkward man who wasn't too good at making funnies, but the punch line never came. Instead, a flash of horror crossed Six's face as though he instantly regretted his confession.

"I need to shower."

Six held up a hand but didn't do anything with it. "Holden—"

"Can you move?"

Six's hand dropped to his side, and his default expression returned. Dead eyes. Blank face. Tight mouth.

He shifted over and sat on the edge of the bed so stiffly it seemed he was the one who'd just been fucked within an inch of his life. Holden scooted off the bed and stood, turning away. Not wanting to see those loosely curled hands. The confession. Or the way the right words had blasted through Six's mental shield and exposed the flood of affection that had been pouring out of him. It could have just been the endorphin rush of his first bang and Holden's schmoopy words, but maybe it was also possible that he'd actually felt something more than an orgasm.

Holden shivered and swiftly walked from his bedroom to the narrow bathroom just down the hall. The heat wasn't turned on, which could have explained his chills, but it was more likely the realization that he was surrounded by a conspiracy. Or in the middle of one? Actively participating in it? He had a lot of questions, but one thing was clear: he'd just had sex with someone who was basically a double fucking agent. Holden hadn't felt any ulterior motives in that postorgasmic glow, but there had to be a reason Six had stayed at the

Farm for all those years, and why he'd taken the job to spy on Holden, when it had nothing to do with devotion or obligation to the Comm.

Once in the shower, Holden tilted his head against the tiled wall and closed his eyes. The water was too hot and the steam was billowing too much for such a tiny space, but he needed Six's touch to be scorched from his flesh along with the memory of that brief connection. Even with the other revelation hanging in the air like a storm cloud, one thing was clear—it was definitely possible to get inside of Six's head.

"Holden."

"Shit!" Holden jerked away from the wall and clapped his hand over his heart. "Don't you fucking knock?"

Six stood on the other side of the shower door, mostly distorted by the steam and the bumpy texture of the glass.

"Can we talk?"

"About Ex-Comm? I'll pass. I already know more than I want to know about that organization."

"Someone told you about it?"

Holden began jerkily scrubbing himself. "Yes. I'm assuming, like the Community, that's a no-no for Ex-Comm. First rule of Fight Club and such."

"Wrong."

Apparently they were back to monosyllable and pulling teeth.

"How am I wrong?" he asked impatiently. "Care to elaborate or do you want to drag this out while you scramble to escape the mess you just created by telling me that?"

"There's no mess," Six said. "Unless you tell your father."

"Does my father even know what Ex-Comm is?"

"Yes." A measured silence followed, as though Six was waiting for a reaction. When Holden just stared at him through the glass without comment, he said, "Your father goes out of his way to extinguish it every chance he gets. That's not an exaggeration, it's the truth. He is fixated on hunting down every member and taking them out, which doesn't work because Ex-Comm is made up of different groups in different places, not one completely unified organization." Six paused, weighing his words, and maybe wondering whether he was saying too much. "Now we can do this two ways—you come out on your own and listen to what I have to say, or I drag you out and make you listen."

Holden twisted the faucet. It turned off with a loud squeal. "Are you threatening me?"

"No. I mean—" Six opened the shower door and squinted at him. At some point, he'd put on his boxers and T-shirt. "Are you being serious? I fucking hate your sarcastic shit all the time."

"That wasn't sarcasm."

"Okay. Then no. I'm not threatening to hurt you. I wouldn't hurt you."

"Why not?" Holden demanded. "I'm the son of Richard Payne. A privileged bastard who has benefited from the exploitation of every Community member who signed the lifetime contract complete with membership fees and blind loyalty. That's the foundation of Ex-Comm's manifesto, isn't it? That the Comm only exists to take advantage of people. Not help them."

"Something like that, but you're oversimplifying it to be a dick."

Even in the middle of a wrenching conversation, there was something undeniably attractive about Six's brutal honestly and steady gaze. Holden stepped out of the shower, naked and unashamed, and took note of the way that same gaze swept over his body. Once, then again. Oh yes—that attraction had been very real.

"I'll listen to what you have to say," Holden said. "But keep in mind that it doesn't mean I'll trade one problematic group for another. I'm not here to take down the Community. All I want is to help my friends."

"And what if you have to take it down in order to help them?"

"You're going to need to explain that hypothetical."

"It's not a hypothetical. It is a fact."

Holden's gut twisted. "How?"

"Come back into the bedroom and I'll tell you everything."

It took over twenty minutes for Holden to sit still enough for Six to start talking. He made coffee, watched a few minutes of NY1, checked his messages, and then finally sat across from Six at the kitchen table. He noticed that Six had yet to touch the gourmet brew.

"Not up to your standards?"

"I don't drink coffee."

"Then why in the hell did you let me pour you a cup?"

"To be polite. It's considered rude for a guest to turn down the offerings of their host."

This was not the time to laugh, but Holden wanted to. Then he felt bad for being amused by Six's social awkwardness. It wasn't his fault he hadn't been properly socialized and that he was literally unable to pick up on the motes of energy that most people used to read another's mood.

Holden grabbed Six's cup and slid it across the table to line up with his own. "I'll drink it."

"That's a lot of coffee."

"It's five o'clock in the morning, and you're about to make a keen effort to get me to betray my father." Holden raised the cup to his lips. "Being alert has its benefits."

Six leaned back in his chair with his thighs spread and hands locked together behind his head. With his hair down, body still flushed from sex, and the lack of clothing, he was devastatingly sexy. It was unfortunate this morning coffee wouldn't result in rejuvenation leading to more sex.

"I don't want you to betray your father."

"No?"

"Unless you want to save your friends."

Holden set his coffee cup down with a *thunk*. "I strongly advise you starting from the top if you expect me to take this conversation seriously. Right now it sounds like the plot of a Marvel movie. Or a dystopian novel. And regardless of my feelings on the way the Community is operating at the moment, I have a filial obligation to not plot against my father. It would take a lot for me to even consider hearing out anything along those lines." When Six cocked his head in apparent confusion, Holden frowned. "Six, do you have parents?"

"No."

"Why not?"

"Because I don't." Six dropped his hands from behind his head to cross his arms over his chest. His shoulders hunched forward just slightly. "Is this the part where you demand to know my sad back story? Try to understand how I lost my way and joined Ex-Comm instead of embracing the nurturing psychic community your daddy founded?"

"Now who's oversimplifying to be a dick?"

Six shrugged. "That's what you're doing, right? I may not feel your vibes, but you're not the first to expect me to have a story just because I'm not the type of person they're used to."

"But you do have a story," Holden said knowingly. "And I only know part of it. That you were picked up by Community Watch as a teenager, but you tried to rob the place and wound up having your life decided for you by a Community tribunal instead of the police."

"The police wouldn't have done the job the board wanted," Six said. "I'd have gotten a month of juvie. Maybe. Your people abducted me. I didn't agree to go to the Farm, but they took me there anyway. And they kept me for *years*."

Holden's hands curled into fists. "You didn't agree to it?"

"No. And even if I had, I was fourteen with no parents and no one to rep me who actually gave a fuck about the choices I was making." Six's lip curled. That, and the glint of his eyes, was the only indication that he felt anything while retelling this story. "And they were a board of powerful psychics in charge of an organization who were *telling* me to go. I didn't think I could say no. I didn't know what they would do to me if I tried. So I went along with it, and I stayed because I had nowhere else to go. And I was scared. It was easy for them to get away with holding me there because they knew no one would be looking for me."

"Where . . . Can I ask about your parents?"

"You can ask, but I don't got any answers for you." Six laughed humorlessly. "Someone told me they were crackheads who dumped me at a church, but there's no real way to know. I grew up a ward of the state, and that got old real fast once my mental shield set in. I was strange and everyone knew it. And it was awful. The worst fucking thing for a kid in a situation like that is to be different. The ability to blend in is protection. It's safer to be no one."

Holden looked down at his coffee cup. The still black pool reminded him of Six's eyes.

The board meeting where Six's fate had been decided had been years and years ago, but Holden would never forget the impression it had left on his younger self. The Community acting as judge and jury, and them never once looking in the direction of the slim young boy with the darting black eyes who sat alone in a corner. If it had scared Holden, he had no idea how Six must have felt at the time.

Something scrabbled at the back of Holden's neck. Invisible feelings trying to grab him by the scruff and pull him away from this conversation and the inevitable crush of sympathy that would lead to Holden staying still, dropping the wise-guy routine, and hearing Six out. But he ignored it and took another swig from his cooling coffee.

Maybe this was dangerous territory, and maybe he should have shut this down and walked away, but everything was ringing true. What they'd done had been abduction. They'd made sure that Sixtus Rossi had vanished from the Earth by keeping him holed up on the Farm for over a decade.

"Why did they want you out of the way?"

"Because I saw something I wasn't supposed to see."

The tingle of knotting nerves that had started in the bed exploded into a full-on creep crawl through his body. Goose bumps spread over him.

"In the CW?"

Six nodded slowly. "I ran away from my group home at twelve. Left with a friend. Meadow." Six looked down at the table as he combed a hand through his hair. "Meadow was a telepath. To this day, she's the most talented telepath I've ever met. And believe me, I've met a lot. We sensed something in each other right off the bat, which is why we were so close. Partners in crime on the run from the system that was likely going to crush us if we stayed in it long enough." He gathered his hair together and tied it in a loose knot. "We never got dragged back to the group home, but we met someone who told us about a safe place for psy kids."

"Who did you meet? Where?"

"There you go with those questions again. That's what always made you so dangerous to the board. And to your father." Six's eyes flashed up at Holden. "We were at a youth center in SoHo. There were Community plants there. Counselors who vetted psy kids and directed them toward the CW."

Holden frowned. There was something uncomfortable about that. Something . . . predatory.

"Yeah, you get it." Six nodded, and the last remnants of his hesitation vanished. "So we went to the CW, and they mostly ignored me and zeroed in on Meadow. They said she was amazing. Incredible. Had so much potential that they wanted her to go to a special camp for special people just like her so she could learn how to really explore her talent. I wasn't invited." He flashed a tight smile. "They took her to the Farm, and I didn't hear a thing about her for months. And nobody would give me answers. So, I decided to look into it myself."

"The robbery wasn't a robbery," Holden said. "You were looking for information about Meadow."

"You got it. I found information on her, among other things." That humorless laugh sounded again, ominous and chilly in the silent kitchen. "Just because folks are big-time psychics, doesn't mean they had smarts about computer security back in the late nineties. All the information was right there on your father's computer. All it took was a few keystrokes to find files with Meadow's name."

Holden stood and began to pace. He knew Six was watching him, but he couldn't keep still any longer. This thing was building and building, and he had no idea where it was going anymore. He had already wrapped his mind around a psychic vampire who'd been twisted by the obscene hierarchy of the Community. But now . . .

"At the time there was a directory of everyone in the Community. They categorized us by psychic power and then ranked us by utility. Those with the highest utility were vetted for the Farm, where they'd undergo evaluations and realignment, and be taught to become devoted staff of the Community."

"I don't get that. Realignment is meant for people who've lost focus. Why would they realign people just because they're extremely talented?"

"Do you think everyone's realignment looked like yours?"

"I—" Did he think everyone got private tutors and gourmet meals? Absolutely not. "Even so . . . it doesn't make sense. The purpose of realignment is like . . . it's supposed to be so people can check themselves and relearn the principles of the Community. The goals and rules."

"Holden, you're repeating this bullshit because you want to believe it. It doesn't make it true."

"Fine. Then what's the truth?"

Six placed both of his hands on the table, palms down, with his fingertips pressing against the flimsy wood. "Your mother has experienced the real version of realignment."

"My mo—" Holden broke off as the sound of her shrill voice rang in his ears along with the robotic defenses of his father. He stopped pacing and put a palm against the wall, steadying himself. "It's brainwashing."

"Correct. A more suitable term would be 'reprogramming.'"

"Jesus God." Holden inhaled sharply but couldn't seem to catch the breath he didn't remember losing. He leaned heavily against the wall. "Is it reversible?"

"I don't know, but some people are resistant to it."

"Like you," Holden said.

"And your brother."

Holden slid down the wall until his ass met the floor. He'd known all along that Chase was at the Farm, but now . . . "Do you think they're trying to reprogram him?"

"Maybe. I saw when they brought him in, but he was kept isolated this time around." Six got to his feet and took measured steps over to where Holden had slid to the floor. There was a moment where indecision appeared to consume him, evident in hands that rose before once again falling to his sides, and the way his mouth opened and closed before he spoke again. "Years ago when I first went to the Farm, your brother was still there. Jasper was continuously . . . working on him. Studying him. And then trying to program him to become a devoted Community member, but he was resistant. Even though he'd grown up in that place, his mind was open enough for him to see it all for what it was. They tried other means of controlling him, like leeching some of his abilities away. They thought that was what finally caused the reprogramming to take effect, but in reality—"

"He was just faking it so they'd stop . . . torturing him." Holden was nauseated. Psychic vampires or leeches or whatever they were called had never been a myth or a legend. The Community had known about them. The Community used them. Used them on Chase and who knew how many others. Maybe Lia had been right about the other disappearances. It was entirely possible Beck hadn't been behind all of them. In fact, it was entirely possible that Beck hadn't acted on her own. At this point, the unlikely and the awful were all possible. "My God."

"Are you okay?"

Holden clenched his fingers in his hair, but it did nothing to stop his racing mind and pounding heart. "How could I have never known?"

"Because you didn't work on the Farm around people who were unable to psy fuck you into forgetting everything you'd seen." Six crouched on the floor beside Holden. He put a tentative hand on his shoulder. "I worked out pretty quickly that it was better to pretend their brainwashing had worked on me, so they trusted me to be a good little cyborg for them. And along the way, I met someone from Ex-Comm right before she was reprogrammed."

"Who?"

Six's gaze cut away. "I'd rather not say."

Holden searched his face intently. "Do Hale and Kyger know, or is this my father's operation?"

"In all my years of working at the Farm, I've never once seen the other founders there. It was only your father. He would talk about his vision for the Community—a place where powerful psy children were born, bred, and groomed to become influential members of society, whether that was as celebrities, musicians, socialites, or politicians. He saw the potential in psychic powers to shape things in a way that would make the Community, and him, a powerful force."

"My father actually made that statement?"

Six nodded. "Not all in one go, but over time. He talked to me a lot even though I didn't always talk back. He trusted me."

Holden shook his head in disbelief. "My father doesn't trust anyone. Not even me."

"Because you ask too many questions," Six repeated. "You're too smart. Too thoughtful. And people like your father consider that threatening. They want you to accept his truth and not wonder what else is missing from the equation."

"And he thought you had done that. That you'd been one hundred percent reprogrammed over time?" Holden leaned forward, brow wrinkling. "But why would they think that when you're completely shielded from psychic manipulation?"

"Because you don't need psychic powers to reprogram someone." A shadow crossed Six's face, and his gaze slanted away. "I do believe they have dreamwalkers and telepaths who might work on people who go in for realignment, and go for a subtle approach, but that's not what happens to people like me. Or Chase. Or your mother. We're too shielded from psychic invasions, so they try the old-fashioned approach."

Holden felt sick, but he didn't interrupt.

"Sensory deprivation, starvation, repeated questioning by different people or people in masks once you're confused and delusional. Exploiting your weaknesses, finding your guilt, and then making you believe that they'll help you get out of there if only you would stop being so difficult. And when they've defeated you, and have gotten you to say what they want you to say, they make you repeat it until it becomes real to you."

"My God . . ."

Holden wanted to close his eyes or cover his ears, but he didn't. He stared into the bottomless pools of Six's eyes.

"They also use drugs. Psy suppressants and sedatives to keep people calm and stop them from utilizing their own gifts."

"Do psy suppressants prevent a psychic from using his shield?"

Six shook his head. "No. A mental shield isn't an extrasensory gift. It's just a way of protecting yourself and finding strength within yourself."

"Except for you," Holden said. "That's different."

"Right. I was born with some kind of psychic immunity."

It was all so wild. So fucking farfetched that Holden wanted to say it wasn't true. That it couldn't be true. That there was no way there was so much evil lurking in the heart of the Community that had been his home.

"Who is the Ex-Comm person you met at the Comm?" he pressed again. "I want to know who else has known about my father."

"It's irrelevant. My original point was that if I'd never met that person, I'd be in the dark just like you."

"Somehow I doubt it." Holden braced his hands against his eyes, wincing, before dropping them again. "For a cyborg, you're good at trying to comfort people."

"Heh. I do okay when I make an effort."

Holden shrugged off Six's hand. "And why are you making an effort with me? Why did you even take this job, Sixtus? Something tells me my father didn't handpick you from the Farm and put you here."

"You're right about that. I was standing by during a board meeting, heard the discussion about the problem with Evolution, and volunteered. Said I wanted to get off the Farm for a change."

"Why?"

Six hesitated, then he pressed his lips together and nodded, as if reassuring himself. "Because you were at the tribunal the day I was sent to the Farm. And when they were done discussing my fate, I heard you ask your father if I would be okay. Literally the only human in the room, maybe even in the whole goddamn city, who gave a shit about my state of mind."

Holden started, eyes opening wide. "You saw me?"

"Yeah, I saw you. Even as a kid, I noticed those big hazel eyes with the golden flecks. And how sad they were for me." Six's mouth jerked to the side in a not-quite smile. It was so strained Holden wondered if Six was forcing it just to make the situation less tense and alarming. "I didn't have a lot to hang on to in the next few years, but I always remembered that. I remembered you. Your pretty face and concerned psy-kid eyes. Your grief . . . for me. Even if you forgot about me later, which I figured you had, you'd cared in that moment."

"I cared," Holden said softly. "I thought about you for weeks. And I still remember it like it was yesterday."

"Why?" Six shook his head, but the guardedness was out of his eyes and he looked open again. "I always wondered why you'd said anything at all. I was nothing, and you were everything."

"You were a kid my age who was being tried like an adult," Holden said sharply. "They talked about you like you were an asset, not a person. It was the first time the Community scared me. I never forgot that moment. Or you."

"And I never forgot you." Six wet his lips, hands curling into loose fists. "And sometimes, when I was alone and waiting for the next person to question me for hours while I stood in the middle of a blank white room with my stomach trying to eat itself, your face and the worry in your voice were the only positive memory I could muster. Because you gave a fuck, and also because . . . it was the first time I'd felt connected to someone. I'd never even had that kind of connection with Meadow."

Holden's heart throbbed before climbing to his throat. "When you say you felt connected . . ."

"For the first time, I *felt* someone else." Six reached up to brush his fingers along Holden's cheek, then down to his jaw. "I felt your sadness. Your fear. Your concern. I have no idea why I felt it with you and not Meadow or anyone else in the world up until then—fuck, up until now—but the spark was there. And that spark got me through a lot."

Holden closed his eyes for a moment, taking deep breaths and trying to push down the building urge to pull Six close to him. To kiss him. Be one with him. Because there wasn't time for that now. And he couldn't believe everything Six said. Especially when he'd hidden all this since stepping foot inside of Evolution. And Holden still had no idea if this was all a game. Clever words used to convince a mark.

"You're why I took this assignment," Six said roughly. "Something was cooking and your name was all over it."

"But it's been years," Holden said, voice pitched low. "You expect me to believe you held on to some speck of intrigue or gratitude for all this time?"

"You don't have to believe me, but it's true." Six touched Holden's shoulder again, gentler this time. "I always wondered if you'd grown up to be just another brain-dead Community drone, but from what I heard, you still had remnants of the kid who asked the wrong questions and noticed the things no one else gave a fuck about. So I took the job."

Holden laughed, but it was tinged with disbelief. "Are you sure it's not because you want Richard Payne's son to join Ex-Comm? I'd make a fabulous resource. Unfortunately, I'm not ready to indict my father before confronting him head-on."

Six's entire demeanor closed off. His face shuttered, spine snapping straight as he got to his feet in one fluid motion and took a step back. Whatever he'd been trying to forge with Holden was over. All it had taken was a single sentence.

"If you go to your father, you'll regret it."

"Why?"

"Because he doesn't give a fuck about you, Holden. You may be his son, but you're just another empath in a big crowd of empaths. You don't stand out. You're not Chase."

If Six had shut down, Holden became a wall of ice.

"We'll see about that."

CHAPTER ELEVEN

Holden slept for only forty minutes because that was all his brain would allow.

Between tossing and turning, he dreamed of his parents. In each dream, his mother had no mouth and his father had a gaping hole in his chest. It was fitting but terrifying, and he jerked awake, remembering things about his childhood that had apparently existed in a dark alcove of his brain for the past thirty years.

Before they'd moved to the apartment in the CW building, they'd lived in an enormous mansion on the Upper East Side, complete with an elevator and servant's quarters. His parents' bedroom had been the size of Holden's entire apartment, and they'd had separate closets. On Holden's tenth birthday, he'd found his mother crying in hers. She'd been standing in front of a row of beautiful dresses while sobbing as if someone had completely broken her heart. He'd asked her what was wrong, and she'd lied through her tears.

"I stubbed my toe," she'd said. *"Don't worry, darling."*

She'd been an accomplished psychic and had blocked any attempts of his to reach out with his gift, and he'd taken her at her word despite the bruises on her arms and her strained expression for the rest of the night. His father had acted like he'd noticed nothing amiss, but after that day, Holden hadn't been able to stop noticing. Suddenly, he found his mother crying or staring blankly or clenching her hands into white-knuckled fists with a frequency that had sunk his stomach.

When he was twelve, he'd snuck out of his bedroom after hearing a heated argument in their mammoth-sized one.

"I don't like this," his mother had hissed. *"This is not who we are. It's not who you are."*

His father had shouted back with frustration evident in every word. *"This was always who I was. I'm doing what we need to do."*

"You don't need to do any of this, Richard. It's sick. And if this was your plan all along for the Community, you're sick too."

Even as a child, Holden had felt the imminent danger crackling in the air. It'd twisted his guts, sickening him so badly that he'd had to bite his lip to keep from crying out at the sharp pain ripping through him.

The last memory had been after they'd moved to the CW. It had been the night before his mother had gone to the Farm. Richard Payne had looked at Holden, smiling coldly, and said, *"Say good night to your mother, Holden."*

Even without knowing what was coming, the ongoing cycle of his mother coming and going upstate before living there indefinitely, Holden had been unsettled by his tone. But he'd been more unsettled by the look on Chase's face. Chase had stared at Richard Payne, arms crossed and lips twisted in a sneer. Whereas Holden had been confused and afraid, Chase had understood.

There had never been a smoking gun buried in Holden's mind, but there were enough repressed or . . . realigned fragments of moments to culminate into ugliness. A fuller picture of his parents' relationship that went far beyond what he'd already known. Something dark and abusive and frightening that had resulted in his mother being sent away and turned into a mindless drone of the Community. Or more accurately: of Richard Payne and Jasper.

Holden wondered if the other founders knew, or if they, like so many others, were caught up in the constantly evolving lie where Richard was the hero of the Community and anyone who questioned him was a danger.

Holden forced himself to get out of bed at ten o'clock. His eyes were so bloodshot he looked like he'd been hot boxing with a joint rather than tossing in his oversized bed. A shower didn't help. Neither did coffee. There was nothing he could do to unwind and get the kinks out of his system when he was slowly coming to the realization that Lia, Elijah, and Six were right.

His father was a monster.

Holden's initial plan had been to storm Richard's office at the CW, confront him with evidence or at least his assumptions based on clues, and ask what the hell was going on. But the more his brain unlocked the pieces that had been carefully tucked away and hidden, the less that plan made sense. Because Six was right.

If Richard would send away his beautiful and talented wife, and the son who had at least four known talents, why would he spare Holden? The mediocre gay one with the troublesome club. The one he was already trying to use as a scapegoat for the fact that some of his own shit was finally floating on the surface.

Pulling out his phone, Holden stared at Nate's number for a long moment before hitting Call. It went straight to voice mail.

"Fuck."

Next up was Lia. Her phone rang several times before also going to voice mail.

"Goddamn it."

Holden paced again, running a hand over his unruly hair. He'd been yanking his hands through it all night, and it was full of snarls. Sitting on the edge of the bed, Holden pulled at the tangles while staring at his phone. Six was the only other option, but would the man even talk to him again after the way their night, morning, whatever, had ended? With Holden icing him out due to an inability to digest the information Six had forced on him, and Six losing patience with Holden's failure to get with the program and stop trying to talk reason with Big Daddy Payne.

And he'd been right to lose patience. Maybe.

Unless this was all bullshit, and Holden was being massively mind-fucked by Ex-Comm as well as the Community.

"Fuck this," he whispered to himself. "I'm doing this my own way."

If Richard Payne had taught him anything, it was that grabbing the bull by the horns was the only way to get things done. In this case, the bull was the Community. More specifically, the staff at the Farm. Everything sinister connected to the property upstate. Everyone who needed reprogramming or punishment ended up there. And it had started at Richard's property, which was likely why the other founders never stepped foot onto it. They seemed to trust him to carry on with his plans and believed every word he said.

How could so many people—intelligent, talented people—be fooled by one person? Were they that desperate for a leader? Someone they could look at as a hero who would save them from a society they'd been groomed to fear? Fear had laid the foundation for so much in the Community. Holden had grown up being taught to be afraid of voids, to not trust the government, be wary of unconnected psys, and to truly believe that everyone was out to get them. He had been raised to believe they all had a special secret and a special mission to protect each other from the rest of a menacing world. But all along the menace had been inside, leading them unknowingly into whatever nightmare had been unraveling at the Farm.

Nobody called Holden back as he changed his clothes and headed out to the nearest car rental place. He was texting Kamryn while filling out the needed paperwork to rent an impressively bland sedan to drive to upstate New York for the day. He was on the road within the hour, but his phone did not ring until he was out of NYC proper and was speeding along the increasingly snowy Taconic State Parkway.

"Holden, where the hell are you?"

"Hey, Kamryn." Holden put the phone on speaker and shoved it in the awkwardly shaped center console. "Going on an unexpected trip. I should be back by evening if all goes well."

He hadn't planned on what would happen if all . . . didn't go well. His only plan so far was to flash his face, drop his name, and act like it was completely normal that he'd shown up asking about his family members and friend.

"'If all goes well'? What's that mean?"

"It just means if I don't get held up."

"I see." She hummed. "You sound weird."

"I'm fine, but thank you for noticing I'm weirder than usual. Is something wrong at the club?"

"The fire marshal is here."

"Fuck." Somehow, in the midst of everything else, that sentence was the icing on the cake. On a good day, fire marshals were pains in the asses. And this was definitely not a good day. All of the doors they wanted to stay unlocked were likely locked, and there were probably objects obstructing pathways and fire extinguishers in all the wrong places. "Are we fined yet?"

"She just started snooping around. I was hoping you could come in and deal with it, but I guess you blew off work to go on a day trip . . ."

"I knew my lovely general manager would be able to handle it," Holden said through a yawn.

"And who might that be?" Kamryn asked. "Because my pay isn't really—"

"If you want the position, it's yours. We can discuss salary when I return."

There was a silence punctuated by loud voices in the background and the fainter murmur of a song. "Holden, is this for real?"

"Yes. You're business savvy, are more responsible than I am, and I'm coming to realize that I can't do everything that's needed to keep the club running. We can hire another bartender—"

"But I like tending bar!"

"Well, then we can hire someone else part-time so you're at least sharing the shifts. Either way, I want you to help me run that damn club. If anything happens to me, there has to be someone—"

"Um. What now?"

Sleep deprivation was making him stupid. Holden tilted his head back against the seat and watched the road through slitted eyes. His head was pounding so powerfully that he could feel and hear the beating of his heart.

"Anything could happen to anyone at any moment. Take my current situation—I'm driving on a bridge while running on forty minutes of sleep. My eyes have shut twice since I started driving. I could end up—"

"Okay, shut up, Mr. Morbid. You're not driving off a fucking cliff while on the phone with me. You better hang up first."

"That's your concern?"

"Well, I don't want you to die, but I also don't wanna go through life having heard the splash of your car falling into a river."

"It's a reservoir."

"Holden . . ."

"Okay. Sorry. I'm in a weird mood, and it's good to hear your voice."

"Right . . ." The background noises fell away, and Kamryn huffed out a long sigh. "As your potential new general manager, is there anything you want me to do today besides scramble around trying to fix things we'll get fined for?"

"Honestly, Kamryn, I can't think right now. Just make sure Six is careful about who he lets in the club tonight." He paused, wetting his lips, and considered his next words carefully. "I've gotten several complaints of men coming into the club and just . . . watching people. And then following them outside. In fact, tell Six *and* Stefen that—"

"Six isn't here either."

"Oh."

"Yeah. He's usually here about six hours after last call even though he doesn't need to be. Maybe he should be your general manager."

"Fuck that. It's you or no one."

"If you keep gassing my head up like this, you may live to regret it."

"Never."

They hung up after Kamryn promised to text him as soon as Six walked through the doors. It *was* strange that he hadn't shown up yet, but there was no way to figure out what to make of it. Either he was sleeping in to commemorate the morning after his first fuck, or he was off taking an entirely different bull by an entirely different set of horns.

There were so many different avenues that could lead to, that Holden went right back to cursing himself for getting close to Six. Even for a moment. There was too much between them beyond mysterious connections and fantastic sex for him to seriously consider why he kept picturing Six nervously sitting on the edge of the bed with his fingers curled up. Feelings and attraction would have to take a back burner. For now.

The Farm was literally in the middle of nothing. Trees swallowed the road leading to the property and surrounded tiny towns distantly dotting the area around it. It was beautiful, especially now that it was covered in a dusting of snow, but the isolated aspect niggled at

Holden. If something happened here, there were no witnesses. No one he could run to and no easy escape. He'd be trapped.

Slowing down, Holden eased the sedan to a stop on the side of the road a quarter mile away from the gates leading to the property.

He was being dramatic. As bad as this all looked, there was still the chance they were all wrong. That the Ex-Comm conspiracy theory was a complicated, well-thought-out plot by a bunch of paranoid psychics with too much time on their hands. Except, that was the complicated explanation. The Community having been turned into a cult by Richard Payne to further his own agendas was the simple one.

Holden put his hand on the shifter, fully ready to move forward again, but couldn't do it. This wasn't his first time on the property, but everything about the area put him on edge the way it never had before.

Easing his hand off the shifter, Holden sat back in the driver's seat. Even with measured inhales and exhales, all attempts to find a trace of the calm confidence that had led to this moment were nowhere to be found. The adrenaline that had coursed through him in the early morning hours, fueled by nightmares and a lack of sleep, had been lulled by the car ride. Now, this felt like a very bad idea.

With his hands on the wheel, Holden closed his eyes and reached out with his gift. At first it was just a channel opening to his own car, but with each inhale and exhale, he expanded the breadth until he could feel everything in the vicinity. As a kid, he and Chase had tested it and determined if he pushed himself, he could pick up on the vibes from people within two or three city blocks. Out in the middle of nowhere, Holden should have picked up on nothing but the pitter-patter heartbeat of animals and whatever lingering traces had been left behind on the road and foot paths over the years.

Instead, there was a fierce pulse coursing through the channel, a turbulent mix of irritation, determination, and confusion, and it was growing stronger with every passing second. As if someone was coming right at Holden.

He dropped his hand on the shifter again and jerked it into reverse before doing a swift U-turn away from the property. The pulse was bigger and brighter with every breath he took, bringing the individual closer to the road where they would see him or at the very least . . . the license plate, which could be linked back to him. Every thought racing through his brain was packed full of paranoia and irrational fear, but if Holden had learned to trust anything in his thirty-some-odd years of being an empath, it was to trust the vibes he picked up from people. And these vibes gave him the same sense of imminent danger that his father had so many years ago.

A couple of yards down the parkway was an off-road path leading into the trees. He veered sharply onto it and sped through the narrow opening just as the pulse burst into a supernova of energy indicating another presence nearby. Instinctively, Holden eased open the driver's door, removed the keys and the papers he'd gotten from the car rental, and scrambled behind one of the towering tree trunks while trying his best to call forth a mental shield that was slightly comparable to the one that made Six invisible. It was absurd to be taking this much precaution, but his gut was telling him to not be caught out in the middle of nowhere on this snowy January day by some of the Farm's security.

Holden peeked around the tree trunk and spotted two people on the road. His suspicions were confirmed.

For years, he'd only thought of the Farm's staff as it had been in his childhood. Dour, homely, and wearing bland uniforms—the types of people who gave their life to an organization like the Community because they didn't have much outside of it. They relied on the routine and dedication of people at the Farm to give them purpose. As a kid, Holden had looked up to them. As a teen, Holden had thought they were fucking losers.

But Six hadn't fit that mold, and neither did the two individuals on the road. It was very clear things at the Farm had changed.

He saw a woman with waist-length blonde hair wearing black leathers, and a man with fiery red hair who wore the same. They were riding the quietest motorbikes Holden had ever seen, and were staring down the road with matching frowns. Looking for him.

Holden's heart sank, and his hands trembled as he gripped the rough bark. He watched them pace down the road while conferring with each other, pointing down the winding parkway that led to the bridge. If luck was on his side, they'd be obtuse enough to think he'd somehow sped away in that brief span of time. But Holden was a lot of things and lucky wasn't one of them.

They both turned toward the side of the road. Panic exploded inside of him and, for just a moment, his shield slipped.

Their heads snapped up like hunting dogs who'd gotten a whiff of fresh blood.

He was fucked.

Holden pushed himself away from the tree and took a careful step backward. His back collided with something hard, and his mouth dropped open in an involuntary scream. A hand clamped over his mouth, yanking him back against a broad chest, and then the thick blanket of an impenetrable mental shield surrounded him.

"Stay quiet and come with me," Six whispered in his ear. "Or you'll end up like your friends."

CHAPTER TWELVE

They abandoned the car and didn't speak during the jog through the wooded area surrounding the farm. With each step and each twig breaking beneath his shoes, Holden cringed. The sounds were magnified by the quiet of the woods, and his failed sense of direction did nothing to tell him whether they'd gotten a good distance away from the road.

He shifted closer to Six, so close he bumped into him several times, but his presence was comforting. The wall of his mental shield felt like protection against the outside world, and Holden craved even an illusion of safety. It slowed his heart rate and allowed him to catch his breath. Once they reached a small cabin tucked into a cluster of trees, he was composed enough to not appear completely hysterical.

"What is this place?"

Six started for the stairs, paused, and then glanced at Holden. "Do you feel anyone?"

Holden blankly stared for a second before comprehension triggered. He reached out with his gift, widening it as far as it could go, and cursed himself for not having done this during their trek through the mix of forests and marshland interweaving throughout the area. His first reaction had been to cling to Six, not find a way to protect himself. That was a problem.

"I don't feel anyone at all," he said. "But it only extends so far."

Nodding, Six climbed up onto the porch and unlocked the door. "Just keep your third eye wide open. There's always a chance someone can shield themselves, but if you could feel the guards, there's a good chance you're more powerful than they are."

"How did you know I could feel them?"

"Because you ran." Six stood in the middle of the small cabin. "Which was smart."

Holden turned the lock on the door handle and looked around. The cabin was cozy in a rustic and outdated way, with cedar wood panels lining the walls and floor, and furniture so faded he could barely see the floral design. There was a tidy little kitchen in the corner of the room and a short hallway leading to another room, but the entire place couldn't have been more than seven hundred square feet.

"What is this place?" he asked again.

"It's where I stayed while working on the Farm." Six turned on a small lamp next to the couch and flooded the room with golden light. "I was one of the few guards who was able to live elsewhere."

"What made you special? The length of time you were there?"

"Yeah. Most guards put in their time before requesting to be transferred to the CW or some other assignment in a city." Six sat on the hideous couch and hunched forward, his elbows on his knees. "Your father let me have this because I never asked to go anywhere else. He wanted me . . . relatively happy, and I appeared brainwashed enough to be happy with this place."

There was enough room on the couch for Holden, but he didn't move. He wrapped his arms around himself and focused on the endless darkness of Six's eyes, wondering how they'd become a source of comfort after weeks of distrust. "Why do the guards have guns, Six?"

"Same reason they do at a prison."

"But this isn't a prison." At Six's sideways look, Holden took a step forward. "It's not."

"On the surface it's not, but I already told you what this place has turned into. You just don't want to believe it."

"Because—" Breaking off, Holden began to pace the room with his hands buried in his hair. "Because this is out of control. I was *raised* in this Community, Six. These people were my family. Growing up, people talked about the Farm and the people who worked there like they were clergy. They were what other members aspired to be, or at least respected even if that wasn't what we wanted. And now you're telling me it's this fucking—" He yanked one hand free. "It's a fucking prison where problematic members are reprogrammed, where talents are leeched, and troublesome psys are tortured. And they, what? They shoot anyone who tries to come in or out?"

"Yes. Allowing a trespasser to see what happens here, or a Community member to escape and expose the truth, is too risky."

Dread swamped Holden. His pulse raced once again. "Have you ever shot anyone?"

Six's dark gaze slid to the window. His fingers tightened into fists. "Yes."

"Oh my God. I'm going to be sick."

Holden turned away to press himself against the window, needing the cold smooth glass to wake him from this nightmare. It couldn't be real. This mounting horror had to be happening in the most twisted depths of his mind. There was no way this was life. No way this was the Community that had uplifted so many. That had raised him.

Without warning, Six's hands slid up over his back to curve around his shoulders.

Holden shouldn't have wanted those hands on him—hands that had hurt and maybe even killed. But he couldn't push Six away. He was drawn in by the strength of him, and when that bubble wrapped around him again, he felt almost safe enough to break. As his chest constricted, he allowed Six to turn him so they were chest to chest.

"I'm not a murderer."

Holden leaned heavily against the window instead of pressing against Six the way his body wanted to. He refused to look up. "You shot someone for trying to leave the Farm. You killed someone."

"I had no choice," Six said fiercely. He gripped Holden's chin and forced him to look up and witness the terrible grief that had shown in Six's eyes. The vacant facade had shattered to expose a sadness so sharp it briefly, just briefly, pinged Holden's talent. "I was a teenager when they put me here and put me through their fucking reprogramming. They put me in a room with no windows, and every day they'd come in and talk about my life. My past. My parents. Where I'd be without the Community. They *hurt* me." He searched Holden's face as the pinprick of his pain emanated from behind his shield. "And they didn't feed me or let me out until I nodded and smiled and agreed. It took them over a year to get me to that point."

Holden slumped against the window, but the powerful grip on his body didn't allow him much space. He could still feel the erratic beating of Six's heart, the pain that grew larger with each word until it throbbed like an open wound.

"Then they started working on my talent. Testing it."

"Testing it how?" Holden asked hoarsely.

"Think of it as a psychic version of probing. I was strapped down and toyed with for months until they were certain I was impenetrable." Six's mouth curled down. "They brought in their most powerful psychics to experiment on me. Including your brother. He refused, and Jasper beat him so badly I thought he would die. I don't know if your father knew about that. Sometimes he wasn't here for months at a time."

Holden's hands shook. He clamped them on Six's upper arms to keep them steady, but there was no stopping it. His entire world was crumbling around him, and the only person with the ability to ground him was the man in front of him.

"So I started to lie." Six shook his head, and the muscles in his shoulders flexed with the movement. "No one knew I fucking hated them all. I let them turn me into their special tool, let them give me a job and a gun, and I did what I had to do while waiting for a way out."

There was a ferocity in him that Holden had never seen before. It pinged more than his gift—it had his desire swarming and his hands tightening. The way his body responded to this man was completely unfair.

"Who did you kill?"

"A nobody like me. A kid they found with no parents and no family. The easiest victim in their eyes. Brought him to the CW, found his telepathy interesting, and dragged him here to poke and prod." Six shook his head, lashes lowering until the shadows of his eyes were obscured. "He couldn't handle it. He wasn't like me. I tried to tell him to hold on, or to fake it, but he couldn't because he could hear every thought they had. He *knew* what their plans for him were, and he wouldn't let them bend him without a fight."

"So he tried to escape."

"No. He knew he wouldn't escape, but he ran while knowing what would happen to me if I let him go."

The weight of truth had already been resting on Holden's shoulders, but that burden intensified. "He wanted to die."

"Yes," Six rasped. "I was only nineteen. And I hated myself. But I did what I had to do in order to survive. To make it. And to one day get out and destroy them all."

The wound of his sadness grew more raw, and Holden felt it like the slide of a dagger penetrating skin and muscle to sink into his chest. Somehow, despite the shield, Six's pain was becoming his own. Holden took it and kept taking as he pulled Six in and wrapped him in his arms. It was an awkward hug. Six stood ramrod straight, his arms dangling and hands limp, until Holden reached for Six's grief with a more powerful grip and opened the channel between their minds. If he was going to take on the burden of Six's sorrow, he would exchange it for his own compassion.

"Can you feel me?"

Six nodded jerkily, eyes opening wider and gleaming with wonder. "How are you doing this?"

"It just happens when I'm close to you. I don't even try."

"That's impossible."

"No." Holden ignored the internal warnings that were screaming that his next words would be the final steps taken before he fell down the hole he'd been trying to avoid. "It's not. There's a connection between us that I don't understand, but it's there."

He didn't know what he'd expected after that declaration, but Six exuded sadness, self-loathing, and a brightening sense of relief. *Relief*. And it was directed at Holden.

"There's something between us," Six said. "I always knew there was. You were different."

"Than who?"

"Than everyone."

Holden looped his arms behind Six's neck and pulled him in for another embrace. He wasn't used to this need for closeness and affection, but he craved Six's warmth. Now, he also craved their connection and tried his best to ease away Six's hurt with the widening strands of his fondness.

"Kiss me," Six rasped.

Shuddering, Holden said, "This is a really bad time for this."

"I don't care. I need you." Six cupped the sides of Holden's face and stared down at his mouth like a man starved. "Please let me feel something besides the anarchy in my fucked-up head."

So that was what this was about. It made sense. And now that Holden could define what was happening and give it a name beyond an unwieldy and quickly spiraling attraction, he stopped resisting the demands of his own body. Crushed their lips together and slid his tongue into Six's mouth with swipes that drew deep moans from the man he was ravishing.

The muscles beneath Holden's hands were like rocks, the scruff against his face prickly—everything about Six was rough and hard. Yet instead of dominating Holden, Six worshiped his mouth. Explored every centimeter of the wet heat, moaning louder when Holden ripped his hair out of the loose knot it'd been tied in, and pressed their lower bodies together after several minutes of tonguing each other into an alternate universe. One where he could teach this impenetrable cipher how to open himself up and feel how much Holden wanted him.

"Can I fuck you?"

Holden's dick went from hard to harder. He yanked Six tighter against him, and felt the wickedly stiff length of an erection against his own. "We're about to be hunted down and dragged off for reprogramming," he uttered. "Do you think it's a good time?"

"I think it's the best time. I could be inside you one more time before we die."

"That's really the last thing you want to do?"

"Yes," Six said in a guttural growl. "And it's not just the sex. When we fuck, I'm sucked into this light. This place made of goodness and happiness. It's the best feeling in the world, and it's because I'm with you."

Holden sucked in a breath. "Maybe it's just an orgasm you're feeling."

"No." Six's voice was a thunderclap, his fierce scowl a storm. "It's you, Holden. You make me feel like someone else. Like someone new."

"Is that a good thing?"

"Yes. I always knew you were different. Special. I just didn't know..." Six faltered, his confusion looking severe despite the softness emanating from his eyes. "I didn't know I'd feel this way about you. The idea of you being hurt made me insane. I got here as fast as I could and the whole time it felt like someone was ripping my heart in shreds because I thought I'd be too late."

No amount of even breathing could calm Holden's stuttering pulse. Six was unlocking a part of him that had long been dormant. The part that craved intimacy beyond sex. That had once, long ago, wanted love. The most dangerous emotion he'd ever encountered and the one that had always scared him the most.

And he wasn't scared now. The vulnerability of this moment, of Six's burning eyes, sent adrenaline buzzing through his veins.

Could this be real?

"For the first time in my life, I don't know what to say."

"Say I can have you one more time before we go back," Six said urgently.

"After that speech, you don't have to ask."

Six's face lit up, as though he'd really doubted Holden's desire. He grabbed the back of Holden's neck, drawing him into a kiss so hard he was left panting and gripping the front of Six's shirt. Together they moved away from the window and down the short hallway. The bedroom they entered was nothing special—a single window covered by long, dusty drapes, a full-sized bed that should not have been able to contain Six's large body, and a battered chest of drawers. It was lonely and a little sad, and Holden had just enough brain power left to realize how much he hated the idea of Six having lived here alone.

"Will we both fit on the bed?" he asked hoarsely.

"We'll make it work."

A small voice in the back of Holden's mind reminded him that this was the worst possible time for a quick and tawdry tryst, but nothing about it felt tawdry or unnecessary. It felt like one last piece of humanity before it all went to hell.

They kissed harder, lips moving more hungrily the more anticipation built. Holden made short work of Six's belt and pants, rucking them down to expose tight briefs straining over his dick. They'd been together twice, but Holden would never get over the size of Six. His mouth went dry at the thought that they'd be doing this with no lube, but the sharp ache of want inside of him overpowered everything else.

He lay on his back and impatiently kicked his pants off. When Six knelt between his thighs with his powerful body on full display, Holden nearly lost it. A sharp coil of pleasure burned through him, ending in a grunt and a trickle of pre-come sliding from his slit.

"Make it as wet as you can get it," he said hoarsely. "And hold me open so I can watch."

Six nodded wordlessly, the dark coals of his eyes zeroed in on Holden's waiting hole. He swallowed visibly, throat working, before putting his fingers in his mouth to gather saliva. He trickled it over Holden's ass twice, rubbing his fingers in the tight pucker and massaging the surrounding nerve endings until Holden was vibrating. It was all so real and raw, so careful and deliberate, and nothing like he'd felt with anyone but the man hovering over him. A man who'd never been with anyone else, but who managed to make this goddamn mind-blowing for Holden. He was quivering like he'd never been fingered before.

"I don't have a condom," Holden said.

"Do I need one?"

"You've never been with anyone, and I'm anal about getting checked."

Six positioned the fat crown of his dick at Holden's entrance. "Was that a joke?"

Holden released a half-hysterical laugh. "No. Please just fuck me."

Six pushed inside of him, and Holden tensed. He'd never been with someone so large and strong and gentle at the same time. And never when danger was pressing in all around them.

"Shit." Holden's eyes rolled back, and he gripped handfuls of the tacky duvet. "Oh fuck, that hurts."

"Too much?" Six asked roughly.

"No. Don't pull out."

Six gripped the undersides of Holden's knees and held them up and open. The view was perfect. If this was the last thing Holden saw before brainwashed psychics came charging through the door, he wouldn't complain. The only thing that made him happier than watching his ass stretch around a girthy dick was seeing the shudders going through a grown man's body because of the pleasure that tightness was causing him. Right now, he had both. And once again, empathic dual fucking wasn't needed. This was all Six.

Six pulled out an inch, pushed back in, and then repeated this process until he sank the remaining way. Holden's body screamed in protest, his ass throbbing, but it mingled with electric currents of pleasure so shocking his eyes watered.

Six moved with deep, sure strokes and shattered the remaining resistance of Holden's body. It gave way to the intrusion and then welcomed it with mind-numbing bursts of pleasure every time Six slammed into him again. The pain didn't vanish, but it was just an edge on the very perimeter of the stunning reality of being fucked open wider than he'd ever been before.

Holden tossed his head back and didn't attempt to swallow the animal-like grunts falling from his mouth. He held his thighs open wider and watched Six power in and out of his body. Cock aching, he was tempted to reach down and stroke it, but didn't. He would do nothing to ruin this view. Not even when Six slowed and nearly pulled out entirely before pushing into him with another clean, sharp thrust.

"Yes," Holden whispered. "Don't stop until you come."

Six hunched forward, hair sweaty and flying everywhere. "I'm close. Jerk yourself off."

"Soon."

Six sank deep again, and his eyes rolled back. "I want to feel this forever," he uttered. "Feel you forever."

Holden's gut twisted. There was no time to process those words. Almost as soon as Six said them, he was steadily pumping into Holden again. His balls swinging, his fingers gripping, he slid into Holden so precisely that Holden was starting to fall to pieces. His toes curled and he began to shudder uncontrollably. He closed his eyes, squeezing them shut as waves of pleasure spread from his sac and radiated through his body, but he couldn't get back the control from even a minute ago.

He couldn't get over how full he felt. How vulnerable it was to be this stretched open, and how unrelenting Six's thrusts were. And then he realized, very abruptly, that he could feel Six in other ways as well.

His pleasure, his dick being milked, and the absolute bliss of being inside Holden.

All of that welled up into a column and shot straight through the connection that had abruptly opened between them. Holden lost his damn mind.

"Oh fuck," he cried out. He moved restlessly, arching up to meet the dick driving into him. He impaled himself faster, wanting more even though he was filled to the core. "Oh fuck, Sixtus."

Six pulled out and jerked once before shooting hot jets of semen all over Holden's still gaping hole. The feel of it pushed Holden over the edge. He grabbed his own erection and pumped frantically until his release tore through him before he was ready for it.

Holden went slack on the bed. He panted wildly without speaking. Six lay next to him and did the same.

The air crackled with tension. Desperate fucking and heat-of-the-moment declarations had a way of making things awkward after the fact. Or that's what people had always told Holden about their trysts and hookups that took a quick turn toward complicated. He'd never experienced it himself. No one had ever confessed deep feelings for him, and he'd always written that off as it being a side effect of him being a pain.

Maybe that had been wrong.

Six had every reason to hate anyone with his last name, and he didn't.

"I want to feel this forever. Feel you forever."

Holden went to the tiny bathroom to wash up and tried not to wrestle with the pendulum of his mind. One side thought this was a prime example of Holden Payne being unable to keep his dick in his pants even during serious situations, but the other side just kept wondering if Six had meant what he'd said. But it wasn't the time for those wonderings. That became even more apparent when Holden's wavering mental shield pinged three distinct sets of impressions in their vicinity.

"Six," he said sharply, rushing out of the bathroom. "Someone's coming."

CHAPTER THIRTEEN

The lingering gaze Six had been gracing him with hardened into icy blankness. With movements too fluid and deliberate to not be practiced, Six flipped off the lights, yanked Holden down into a crouch, and popped a panel in the floor of the living room to remove a handgun. The sight of it should have been terrifying, but Holden inched closer to Six. He no longer had doubts that the man who'd just fucked him into a blinding orgasm was utterly dangerous, but that was starting to feel like a good thing. His own prowess was limited to dexterously switching subway cars while carrying a Starbucks and his cell phone.

"Stay down," Six whispered. "If I start shooting, try to get to the back room without being seen. There's a window you can fit out in the bedroom."

"What about you?"

Moments ago, the cabin had been full of panting breath, groans, and the humidity created by two sweaty bodies moving against each other. Now the sound of Six cocking the gun was deafening.

"I'll be fine."

"What does that mean?" Holden wrapped his fingers around Six's forearm. "I'm not leaving you here to be caught by those assholes on the road."

"I know those assholes on the road," Six said roughly. "And if I can't reason with them, I'll take care of them."

"You'll kill them."

"I'll do what it takes to keep them from seeing you or contacting the base and saying they've seen me."

"No."

The look Six speared through him was so furious Holden half expected to be wrestled toward the back bedroom. Crouched and coiled with a gun in his hand, Six was frightening. Deadly. But the invisible tunnel of Holden's gift was still sliding through Six's shield, and he could feel how scared Six was. For him. The only threat was coming from the Farm and the Community.

"Listen to me," Holden hissed. "I'm still Richard Payne's son. If anything, I can—"

"*No.* Your fucking privilege doesn't work here, Holden. It's a different world. And you have no reason to be in this cabin or to even know that it exists." Six grabbed a handful of his shirt, yanking him closer and dropping his voice. "If they find you here, you're going to end up like your mother. She wasn't exempt either."

The thought of his mother nearly sent Holden surging to his feet. The tremors started again, making it undeniable that he wasn't cut out for this, but the throb of three different sets of impressions were growing closer, and there was no time to debate anymore.

Six clutched the gun, sitting on his haunches and waiting with efficient movements and measured breaths. He'd always struck Holden as a man who got things done, and that was even more apparent now. He'd get this done if it didn't go their way.

The door opened, and Six started to ease around the corner. There were a thousand thoughts racing through Holden's mind about how this would go and how he would react after seeing his new lover kill a man, maybe three men, but familiarity soared through his open channel. There was a distinct mix of impatience, mounting anxiousness, and exasperation flooding through the connection he'd opened.

Just as Six raised the gun, he grabbed his forearm. "Wait!"

Six gave him a wild look, but Holden ignored it and the hand grabbing at him to jump to his feet. He was utterly unsurprised to be face-to-face with Lia's intense frown, Nate's flustered gaze, and the way Trent clearly thought everyone was doing the absolute most. With his shaggy dark hair and blue eyes, he was extremely pleasing to look at, but Holden had a hard time doing so considering their previous encounter had been with Trent mind controlled and trying to strangle him. Now, Trent glanced at him curiously. That changed into alarm once Six stood up with his gun pointed at Nate's face.

"What the fuck?"

"Put your gun—"

"Oh for Chrissake." Lia stood between Six and Nate with her hands up. "They're cool. Put the gun down."

"'Cool,'" Six repeated flatly. "You're not the authority on who's cool and who's not, and nobody told you to bring extras here."

"Extras? I didn't realize we were on a movie set."

Nate elbowed Trent in the side. He looked different in a pair of cuffed shredded jeans, a faded trench coat, and a bunch of multicolored scarves, but his subtle Texas drawl was the same. "It's really not the time."

Trent crossed his arms over his chest. "Holden, tell your boy to calm his tits."

Holden shook himself. Nate bursting into his life without warning for the second time in a year was just as startling as it'd been the first time. How had he never noticed the similarities between his and Chase's white-blond hair and silver eyes? Those fine features and willowy builds? It was almost as though he'd gone through life in a mist of obliviousness when he hadn't been burying his head in the sand.

"They're with us," he said. "Nate and Trent were the ones who figured out what was going on at the club."

"You mean we figured out that your pops' lady friend was snatching up psychics under your nose," Trent corrected.

Holden set his jaw. "We're all on the same side."

"Are we?" Lia asked. "You're sure this time?"

"I'm sure."

"Excellent." Lia strode across the room and put a hand on Six's tense arm. Slowly and carefully, she pressed it down until the gun was lowered but still clenched in his white-knuckled grip. "Then we can figure out how the hell we're getting onto the Farm."

There had been few times in Holden's life when he'd felt as out of control as he'd been in the past several months. After three decades of thinking he had things well in hand, the current stream of events had turned him into a bundle of exposed nerves. On edge. Jumpy. And bracing himself for what would happen next to jolt his system and turn everything inside out all over again.

He was coiled tight as they settled in the living room with the lights off, the door bolted, and his and Nate's internal antennas up and ready to pick up on unwanted guests. So far so good. Holden felt nothing but the four other people surrounding him, and he could tell by the pinched expression on his lovely face that Nate was struggling with his inability to access Six. He was apparently still impenetrable to everyone but Holden.

Six was standing across the room with his arms folded and his gaze on the window, not trusting their empath talents or Lia's low-tier precog abilities to see what was coming. The cold displeasure etched into his face made for a tense atmosphere, especially because Trent stayed as far away as possible with his body angled in front of Nate. Nate, who was Six's polar opposite in every way, and whose presence emphasized Six's height, brawny muscles, and onyx eyes.

"I gave Nate and Trent a rundown of what's happening," Lia said.

"What was your rundown?" Holden asked. "I'd like to hear the full version."

"You already know it, and Six had to have told you the rest." She leaned against the door, a human barrier to match the flimsy wooden one. "The Community's shit is finally floating to the surface. The situation at Evolution made a lot of people start asking questions and voicing their discontent about the answers given. When it comes down to it, the Community had always relied on gaslighting and intimidation to keep people in line. But you can't send the entire Comm to the Farm for realignment." Lia jerked her chin at Holden. "They needed patsies. And that's Chase, and that's Elijah, and that might even be you. If the overall Community thinks you guys are to blame, then there's no need to question anything else."

"What I don't understand is the end goal." Nate slid his hands into the pockets of his trench coat, drawing it closer around his narrow body. He looked like a movie star with his wind-blown hair and upturned collar. "Why did your dad want Beck to spot rare talents?"

Everyone looked at Holden. Even Six. Was this a test to see how much he'd accepted of the Ex-Comm narrative? They needn't waste their time.

"It seems like my father's real purpose with the Community is to cultivate a group of people who have the psychic capabilities to influence change on a national scale."

"'Change,'" Trent repeated. "Government change?"

"Yes. Maybe? I don't know the details, but it's . . . It really does seem like he's using the CW to cherry-pick people they can suck in and program to further their overall agenda. Anyone who doesn't serve a purpose in that specific agenda just becomes a pawn." Swallowing the bitter pill of his own role, Holden cracked his knuckles and continued. "As Richard Payne's idealistic gay son, my purpose is likely to make it seem like social justice runs in our veins. I care about LGBT issues, and he makes it seem like I get that instinct to care from him. Chase and Six are tools my father could use to safeguard their secrets due to both their uncommon talents and no-nonsense demeanors, and psys like Elijah seem to hold the lowest rank. The CW *does* work with the Elijahs, but mostly so the Elijahs can then give lip service about how much Richard Payne and the Community has done for them. Word of mouth is imperative for this kind of scheme to work."

Six had begun nodding with each word. By the end of Holden's speech, he'd moved to stand beside Holden at the counter. To everyone else, it likely appeared unconscious. Holden knew it meant something else. That theory solidified when Six's hand dropped out of sight and his fingers brushed Holden's palm. If the question had been a final test, Holden had just passed with flying colors. He hadn't even realized how much he'd needed Six's complete trust, but now that he had it, it sent blood coursing through him with the pounding of a drum.

There was something between them all right. He just had no idea what it was.

"Are the other founders involved in this?" Nate asked. "Or just your father?"

"From what Ex-Comm has seen," Lia started, although she raised her hands as if to caution it wasn't one hundred percent, "Hale and Kyger may have an inkling about what's been going on at the Farm, but they're afraid of Richard. Even if they started as equals, it quickly became clear that Richard Payne is the one who holds the power."

Holden glanced at Six to see him nodding in agreement with this assessment. For some reason, it brought a measure of comfort. They weren't all bad. It wasn't all a lie.

"Do they know about Jasper?" he asked.

Lia and Six looked at each other again before Six said, "I don't think they're . . . allowed on the Farm. Richard bills it as Community property, but it's very much his domain. And they let him handle it because they'd rather focus their attention on the CW than what Richard does to handle unruly psys and troublemakers."

Holden shook his head in disgust. Spineless cowards. Even if they weren't involved directly, they were certainly bystanders.

"Why do they let him do this?" Nate demanded, looking incredulous. "He's just one man."

"All it takes is one man," Trent said. "One man who can say just the right things to appeal to people's basest fears, and to reassure them that he can protect them and save the day."

"He's right," Lia said. "And Richard has been the mouthpiece for the founders since the Community started. He's always been the one fanning the flames of how everyone is out to get psychics, and how only the Community can protect us from the voids. In reality, he wants to use us to take control of both the Community and the voids."

"The sick thing is," Six said slowly, "is that he believes the things he says. He doesn't see himself as evil. He thinks he has to be the one to make the tough decisions to save us all from the government and the voids. He has to pick and choose who will be a fighter in his battle to slowly take control, and he has to be the one to snuff out any potential traitors. In his mind, this is all for a greater good that only he sees and understands."

Holden curled his hands into fists until his nails cut into the soft flesh of his palms.

"What's the plan?" Trent broke the brief silence with the impatience and tenacity of a true New Yorker. There was no marinating in the comforting silence that followed the realization that everyone was finally on the same page. He wanted to know what the next step was. "Bust in, get Chase and Elijah, and help them go dark?"

"Hiding worked for us for the past several months," Nate said. "But no one was looking for us. It's different this time."

"It is different, but you all need to be aware of the fact that if we bust onto the Farm, it's going to be war." Six set his gun on the counter. "Even if Hale and Kyger aren't entirely on Richard's side, they'll come for us, and we'd have to destroy them."

"Wait—is that your ultimate goal?" Every time Holden thought he had an idea about where this was all going, there was a new twist or turn with an unexpected outcome waiting for him. "How would you go about doing something like that?"

"There are plans," Lia said vaguely. "It's been in discussion for years."

"Discussion. In Ex-Comm?"

"Ex-Comm isn't one unified group like you seem to be thinking. It's like separate offshoots of former Community members who share the same goal and communicate remotely."

"Like the hacker group Anonymous?" Trent asked. "Different sects operating separately but with a common goal."

Lia nodded. "Yes. Ultimately, most people who think of themselves as being Ex-Comm want to take the Community down."

Judging from the lack of surprise on Nate's and Trent's faces, they knew what Ex-Comm was. Maybe they even knew about this plan to save the psychic world from his father, but Holden was still left feeling like a gay club owner being thrust into a thriller-esque adventure that he was very ill prepared to embark upon.

"What are the plans?" Trent asked. "If you expect us to be involved . . ."

"Nobody expects you to be involved at this point," Six said. "The safest thing for you would be to disappear when this is all said and done."

Lia checked the window like Six had been frequently doing for the past several minutes. Maybe she thought discussion of their secret anti-Comm group was an incantation that would summon the guards. And, hell, maybe it was. It was quickly becoming apparent that there was far more about the world than Holden had ever known.

He sat down on one of the stools at the counter, and was surprised when Nate put a hand on his shoulder.

"You're fine," Nate said quietly. "I don't know what's going on either."

"That's actually comforting."

"I figured it would be. That's why I told you." Nate squeezed his shoulder, totally ignoring the deadly frown Six was aiming at him. "Get in, get Chase and Elijah, and get out. Do we have a way to transport them out of the area?"

"I have a truck hidden farther down the parkway," Six said, still glaring at DEFCON 1. "Depending on the condition they're in, it shouldn't be hard to get them out. I know all of the pathways from the Farm and into the surrounding forest and marshes. Marshes are the best bet since most people stay away and won't be able to easily navigate their way through, but there's also a lake we can row across if things get heated."

"And if we have to split up?" Trent asked. "I was born in Brooklyn, man. I don't mess with marshlands and *Lord of the Rings* shit."

He really was irritatingly likable. He and Nate both were, and it was a relief to have them nearby.

"I have maps in the bedroom unless someone's been messing around in here since I left," Six said. "One has each potential route in and out of the Farm highlighted."

"So you've been preparing for this for a while," Trent said.

"For a decade."

"What happened a decade ago?"

Lia tensed, which was Holden's first clue that there was something bigger at stake here. When Six's attention skipped from Trent to Holden and stayed, his stomach did a dolphin flip. He almost didn't want to know. But that was cowardly, and there was no room for craven bullshit when they were about to storm his father's compound.

"What?"

"Sixtus, this isn't the right time—"

Six cut Lia off with a sharp shake of his head. "He needs to know."

"Know *what*?" Holden demanded.

"That ten years ago I met Jessica Payne. Your mother had just started forming what we now call Ex-Comm."

Holden released a low laugh that ended with a *humph*. It had to be a joke, and not a terribly funny one, but he was the only one laughing. Lia's expression was completely still, Nate was deeply frowning, and Trent half turned away with his hand in his hair as if he was experiencing secondhand embarrassment due to Holden's cluelessness. His smile faded.

"You can't be serious."

"I'm serious."

Holden gritted his teeth. "This isn't the time for your literal replies, Sixtus. Don't fuck around with me."

"I'm not." Six raised his hands and put them down before glancing around the room. The sharp edge of frustration in him was a reminder that he didn't always have the words or the actions to make things right. He didn't know how to break this news smoothly. "I met your mother when she first came to the Farm. Back then it was voluntary. I could tell she was on a mission to make some changes and get through to people being held there. Which is what she did for me."

"How?"

Six's mouth tightened again. "We can talk about the specifics later, but she helped me see there could be more to my life than what I was given by the Community. And then she told me about other people like her who saw the truth about Richard's need to control us, and who wanted to make changes. They just couldn't do it out in the open."

Holden glanced at the others. If it weren't for the knot forming in his throat, the contrast of Nate's rapt expression and Trent's skeptical one would have been hilarious. Maybe it was hilarious. It seemed like everyone knew more about his family than he did. Years of embracing this community the Paynes were said to have cultivated, and everything was a lie. His childhood, his parents—everything. Lies.

"Holden, it's true," Lia said softly. "Your mother is pretty much a folk hero for people in Ex-Comm. And I know that sounds fucking ridiculous, but it's real. She was the one who started slowly unraveling this vow of loyalty that had ensnared everyone. You should know more than anyone that breaking the Community's policy of silence is *huge*."

"It is." Nate's voice pitched lower and his drawl sharpened. "Not being quiet is what got my brother killed."

"And Jericho." Lia flinched when she said his name, like it caused her physical pain to be reminded of his murder. Holden didn't blame her. For months, he'd relived that scene every time he closed his eyes. Sleep had eluded him until very recently. "But your mother saw the truth before anyone, and she wanted to change things. It was why she decided to go to the Farm instead of staying in the city with your father. For years, she put in a lot of work there, but the people she was working on started speaking a little too loudly."

Six nodded. "Yes. Jasper and Richard caught on, and instead of being treated as an executive staff member, she was treated like a community member in need of reprogramming."

"You saw this happen?" Holden asked.

"Yes. And I couldn't do anything to stop it but reach out to others and warn them that she was in trouble."

"Which is why, over time, the conversations among the different Ex-Comm groups shifted from rescue operations to takedowns." Lia looked at Six for confirmation and nodded when she got it. "Before things went down at Evolution, me and a couple of Ex-Comm guys in this area were planning to get your mother out of the Farm. The problem is that we can't tell if she's fully reprogrammed or faking it. She may put up a fight."

"It's possible." Holden pushed away from the counter. He sucked in a shaky breath as her shrill cries echoed in his ears. "She's not herself anymore."

"Can't a telepath get through to her?" Trent asked. "Or a, y'know, dreamwalker or some shit. Like, access the unconscious part of her brain that isn't being controlled."

Lia arched a brow. "If I knew a dreamwalker, it might be possible. That was surprisingly inventive for a void."

"Yeah, well, JLo was looking pretty hot in *The Cell*."

A surprised laugh popped out of Lia's mouth and Nate's mouth twitched in a fond smile, but Six's attention was fixed on Holden. The scrutiny was too much combined with all there was to process.

"I need to think," Holden said. "Is it okay if I go sit outside?"

"No—"

"Yes," Lia interrupted Six. "Get some air. We'll start looking at the maps."

"Good." Holden turned away without looking at any of them. "I'll be back."

"Holden."

He paused just inside the hallway, but Six didn't say anything more. And Holden wanted him to. As confused as he was, and as lied to as he felt, he craved the crackle of Six's protective energy. But it didn't happen, so Holden strode down the dark hallway and found the narrow doorway leading to the back of the cabin. Trees shrouded the area in a way that was likely beautiful in the autumn or spring, but now the leafless sentinels just made the great wooded area eerie.

Holden sat on the edge of the back steps and crossed his arms. He searched for a warmth in himself that would chase away the chill of his fear and the unknown, but the cold had seeped down to his bones. It was entirely possible he would never warm up again.

"Hey."

"Nate," he said without looking up.

"Can I sit with you?"

Holden laughed humorlessly. "Of course."

The back porch was so narrow that Nate's knee and thigh brushed his own as he sat down. A few months ago, Holden would have reached out with his gift to get inside the other empath's head. It'd been like an addiction every time he was around Nate—the cynical untrusting empath from the infamous Black family with the old eyes and sweet mouth. Now, that desire was gone. In fact, that need to know what other people were feeling had begun to fade in the past several weeks. Being closer to Six had forced him to find other ways to communicate beyond searching someone's energy before coming up with an appropriate response.

"How are you dealing with all of this?"

"Do you really care how I'm doing, Nate?"

"You kept your word and didn't bring me or Trent to the attention of your father." Nate half turned toward him and leaned forward.

"I didn't know what to expect from you, which is why I . . . didn't return your call and reached out to Lia instead. I was just scared. But you didn't throw us under the bus even after they tried to use you as a scapegoat. So, yes. I care."

The iron bar sliding down Holden's back softened just a bit. He hunched forward with a huff. "I didn't know I'd needed to hear that until you said it."

Nate's smile was almost triumphant. "I've been practicing my empath skills."

"Oh? No longer scorning your gift?"

"Nope. I'm making my living by reading tarot cards. It requires me to constantly read people's reactions."

Holden tsked. "You're better than that."

"Am I?" Nate wrapped in on himself, elbow resting on his knee and face cradled by his hand. "When I was younger, I used to judge people in my family who read palms or tarot cards. Thought it was a bunch of hocus-pocus and scams. But, after doing it for a while, that's sort of changed." Nate chewed on his lower lip, gaze unfocusing as his thoughts went somewhere far away. "Now it's sort of . . . nice to be able to give people an unbiased perspective about their lives."

"An unbiased perspective." This time, Holden did laugh. "Is that what you're calling it?"

"Yes. Sometimes if the impressions are strong enough, I can see into their thoughts and feel what they felt in the past, and I just sort of . . ." Nate waved his hand. "Read the cards based on what I've felt about their lives and give them my unbiased opinion on what I think they should do. And yes, I know how that sounds. Sometimes I suspect Trent thinks I've turned into a new age hippie with delusions of grandeur."

"Yes, well, that's one way of putting it."

Nate shrugged, smiling slightly. "Don't think I haven't noticed the way you didn't answer my question. *How are you?*"

Holden had hoped the distraction had been sufficient, but he didn't fight for another way out of the conversation. "I'm awful, Nate. Everything I thought I knew about my life is a lie. My father is a monster, my mother . . . he crushed her and her spirit at this place just because she didn't want to accept his corruption of the Community.

There aren't sufficient words in my vocabulary to explain just how not okay I am right now."

"I get it."

"How could you get it? I mean, seriously."

"Because you were right about my family being batshit." Nate sat up straight again, his pale hair tumbling over his shoulders as a dry wind cut through the woods. "I don't think me and my brother were a fluke. I think my family had practiced incest for a while to keep the psychic gifts strong in our genes." Nate's tone was matter-of-fact, as though he'd long accepted this truth. "End result is a family where mental illness and addiction runs rampant due to all the inbreeding, and my mother running here to find solace and instead finding your father. You'd think that would have been the worst for her, the experimentation and them taking Chase, but when she went back to Texas, her own sibling decided to start up the inbreeding again." Nate's lips turned up in a way that showed he'd mastered the art of the humorless smile. "So, I found out my uncle is also my and my brother's father. It's really no wonder she fucking killed herself, if that's what really happened."

Holden was struck silent for so long, with his eyes rounded with shock and awe, that Nate finally cracked a real smile.

"Don't feel like you have to say anything. There's no real way to respond."

"No. There's not." Holden ran his fingers through his hair and exhaled slowly. "But, Jesus, Nate. I suppose you really do understand."

"Yep. Lucky me." Nate pressed his hands against the step to push himself up, but he didn't move. "This is awful, Holden. It's fucking awful. All of this. And I'm sorry your father is so involved, but like I said . . . I know a little bit about the goddamn betrayal of realizing the man you grew up with is actually a monster. Your father is just a different kind than my own." Those silver eyes flashed. "What I've come to realize, and a lot of it has to do with being with Trent, is that just because we're born into something doesn't mean we have to be part of it. We don't have to rationalize it or defend it or take it on our own shoulders. The Black family's shit isn't on me. It's not my shame. And the Community's crimes aren't yours. We can be free of this,

Holden. There's no such fucking thing as fate. We can make our own way and find other people to start over with."

Holden's wall of grief cracked just a little, and Nate's encouraging smile splintered it the rest of the way. He breached the space between them and drew Nate into a loose hug. No vibes. No talents. Just the solid weight of a body against his own and arms around his neck. Who knew it could feel so good just to be close to someone? It wasn't something he'd ever attempted before being with Six.

The thought must have summoned him, because as Holden pulled away from Nate, Six appeared in the back door.

Relief flooded Holden. He realized just how keenly he'd wanted Six to follow and comfort him, but it faded at the serious expression on that hard face.

"I'll be inside," Nate said, excusing himself. "Helping Trent figure out how to navigate trees."

Holden tried to force a smile, but it was wobbly and faded entirely once Six came over to him.

"What's wrong now?"

"I don't like it when he touches you."

Holden's brows snapped together. "What? Who?"

Six jerked his head in the direction Nate had gone.

"Are you serious?"

"Have you known me to joke?"

"I haven't known you to be irrationally possessive either." Holden stared in wonder, unable to hide his surprise. This was one of the more unexpected conversations he'd ever had. "He was just being nice. I mean, have you seen his boyfriend? You're similarly tall, dark, and gorgeous."

"I don't give a shit." Six remained towering over Holden, the air around him crackling with possessiveness and anger. "I don't like it."

Holden grabbed the hem of his coat and dragged him down. At first Six resisted, but he eventually allowed himself to be drawn down onto the step. When Holden shifted closer and cupped that stubbled face with his fingers, breath catching at the way Six leaned into the touch, he had to force himself to not use his newfound ability to read Six. Even if he had the key to unlock all that armor, he refused to abuse it. Because this—the feel of skin and breath and the smolder of bottomless black eyes—was enough.

"You want me to be straightforward with you, so now it's time for you to do the same for me," Holden said. "Tell me what you're thinking."

"I'm thinking about how much I hate this." Six reached up to encircle Holden's wrists with his hands. "When I took this assignment, it was because I remembered you from the tribunal and because you were Jessica's son. I wanted to protect you if I could. Wanting to kiss the fuck out of you every ten minutes wasn't part of the plan. And neither was wanting to be the only one who gets to touch you."

Holden slowly nodded, pulse picking up but unwilling to interrupt this flow of speech.

"I'm sorry I kept secrets from you, but we only just started opening up to each other. And I'm sorry I can't be like Nate—fucking knowing what to say, when to say it, and how to touch you when you need someone to make you feel better." Six wet his lips, a nervous gesture that still drew Holden's gaze. "I've never done this before, so I don't know how to put it into words, but I want to be more than the cyborg bodyguard you're fucking who can also take care of anyone who looks at you sideways. The compassion and comforting words—everything he just did for you—should have come from me. I just don't know how to do it."

"That's not true."

Six pulled Holden closer, strong fingers digging into slumped shoulders. "No. I really don't."

"Give yourself some credit, Sixtus. You're doing a goddamn fine job right now." Holden allowed himself to melt onto Six as if the strings holding him up had been cut. Strong arms encircled him, and the ghost of a smile graced his lips. "If we make it out of this, I can't wait for us to figure out how to be in a relationship. It should be a mess."

"*When* we make it out of this," Six rumbled in his ear. "I may not understand soft touches, but I have the rest of this shit on lock."

"I hope so."

CHAPTER FOURTEEN

It was amazing how easy it was to cope with being overwhelmed and frightened when his lover was standing in front of their ragtag group with a map and a scowl. Holden wasn't sure when his brain had switched over from calling Six *the cyborg* to *his lover*, but the phrase came with absolutely zero alarm.

There were no labels yet attached to their transition from handler and boss's son to wary comrades to comrades who calmed down by making each other come, but Holden didn't need any. Out of all the men he'd ever been with, no one had ever expressed so much frustration over an inability to show him *more affection*. It just didn't happen. Usually, people expressed frustration because they couldn't use him as a stepping stone to greater things in the Community. Holden had never been on the receiving end of a mushy declaration, but he'd just gotten one from a man whose brain prevented him from having empathy. It had to mean something.

"Holden, you with us?"

"You said there are three routes away from the Farm and back to Highway 82," Holden repeated.

"Yes." Six flashed him a tiny smile, like he knew his voice almost always sounded too harsh. That speech out in the yard had definitely meant something. "We have three vehicles at our disposal. Holden left his sedan just off 82 in the woods before Turner Road, I left my motorcycle at the end of Turner at the start of the marshes, and Lia's truck is . . ."

"It's off the road on the property across the highway a ways down," Lia said. "It looks like some kind of government facility and seems to be closed for the holidays. It's probably the farthest vehicle, so whoever goes with me will hopefully be in decent physical condition."

Trent rocked back on the balls of his feet. "Are we expecting them to be injured? I thought it was just brainwashing. Reprogramming. Whatever the hell you're calling it."

"Usually it is," Six said. "But that changes when people aren't cooperative or if they try to escape. And if any of them are too far gone, they may resist and become combative."

"Do you think that will be the case?" Nate pressed.

"I don't know. Elijah hasn't been there long enough to have been thoroughly brainwashed. And Chase is strong-willed and a pain in their asses, so he's likely not fully changed over just yet."

Six glanced down at the map. It outlined the five main buildings on the property—an unused barn, the farmhouse where most staff lived, the guest house, the cottage, and then the silo.

"I'm assuming Jessica is either in the main house or in the guest house, which is where I last saw her. Elijah is probably in the cottages where they do the actual realigning the way it's described to the masses." Six pointed at the dark *X* he'd drawn to mark the silo. "Chase is here."

"They keep him in a grain silo?" Trent asked dubiously. "It has to be converted into something else."

"It is."

Six removed his phone from his pocket and thumbed at it for a moment before passing it around. At some point during his career at the Farm, he'd captured several pictures of the interior of the silo. It had been reconstructed into a four-story building with a freight elevator that went up the middle and tube-like rooms that were packed onto each floor.

"That reminds me of that Japanese tower," Trent said, handing phone back. "The capsule tower."

"That was Richard's inspiration. I was there when they talked about it, and I watched it be built."

"Sounds like you have a lot of history with these people." Nate had unwound his multitude of scarves and shed his trench coat. He looked more familiar in the tattered jeans and a plain white tee. "Are you sure they weren't expecting you to defect all along?"

"I'm positive. Richard wouldn't have let me off the Farm."

"But why was he so sure of himself?" Nate pressed. "I know I'm being cynical, but I like to prepare for the worst. What are the odds that one of their precogs saw this coming and all of this is a giant trap?"

Not having thought of that angle, Holden's stomach clenched. He exchanged looks with Lia, who had shifted closer to Nate. Although he'd known Lia longer, she clearly had a lot of respect for the remaining Black twin. Probably because he'd seen through all the Community bullshit from the get-go. It was hard not to feel a little bitter about having not seen through it as well, especially when Holden's blindness had nearly resulted in catastrophic failure and death.

It was still difficult to look at Trent without remembering his vacant eyes and his strong hands wrapped around Holden's throat. Beck's ability to mind control had been like nothing he'd seen before, and he often wondered which psy she'd cannibalized to absorb the power.

Six set the phone on the counter next to his maps—both real and drawn. He planted his hands and leaned forward, looking between them.

"I don't expect any of you to trust me one hundred percent. If you do, you're probably an idiot."

"I guess I'm an idiot, then," Holden said.

Six's mouth twitched up at the side. "Not you. But these two barely know me and their questions make sense, so I'll put it to them like this—psychics are assholes. They're so caught up in their X-Men shit—"

"See? X-Men," Trent muttered to Nate. "I'm not the only one thinking it."

"—that they stop using their other senses and their instincts. They rely on their abilities or the abilities of people they think they can trust. Because I'm an impenetrable, they can't get that far with me. All they know is what I tell them, because they don't know how to read me any other way, and I've been doing this so long they have no reason to believe I'm not really on their side. And I've never been on their side."

"You know I believe in you, Six," Lia said. "But do you really think we can pull this off? Just walk onto this place, a place three out of five of us have never even been in, and remove three high-profile

Community members? No offense, but if you get me killed, I'm going to whoop your ass in whatever afterlife we end up in."

Now *that* was a question that had reoccurred in the back of Holden's mind since they'd started pointing at maps and going over backup plans, but he'd never voiced it. Maybe he really was an overly trusting idiot, because when Six had confidently outlined how they would get in and out, Holden hadn't doubted that it could happen. Unless they got split up and he was left on his own.

"We can do it," Six said. "You just have to make sure you stay low. This isn't some bustling place where you can blend in. It's quiet, orderly, and everyone knows each other."

"And if someone tries to stop us?" Holden asked. "If someone sees me?"

"Bullshit your way out of it or run."

They waited until nightfall to make their way to the Farm. Good for concealment, but bad for Holden's sense of direction and nerves. With each step, he imagined the crack of a twig or crunch of a dead leaf alerting nearby predators. Previously, he'd thought woods were full of dangerous animals and serial killers. That was potentially the case here, but he was more worried about the guards who were apparently trained to view Comm members as objects to be destroyed or silenced if they didn't perform as expected after all of the conditioning.

According to Six, they always had at least twelve guards on a patrol shift at a time. The upside was that the property was huge, so twelve people couldn't sufficiently patrol the Farm and all four buildings without there being huge gaps in coverage. The downside, to Holden, was that their plan didn't account for any psychics who might sense their presence on the property. Although, all of them except Trent could shield themselves from probing psychic mental fingers. It was a huge chance they were taking, but their hope was that none of the guards would expect a void to stage a daring escape and wouldn't be looking out for those kinds of vibes.

The other thing that bothered Holden was how arrogant his father had to have become to have security this lax. Over the years, his father's feet must have permanently left the earth as he'd started thinking of himself as a small god lording over the community he'd created. The *cult* he'd created. And they were so sure of their reprogramming, they'd clearly never expected the lack of security to ever become a problem. The real problem was whether that arrogance was valid.

Holden's mother had been an entirely different person on the phone. If it hadn't been an act, it would be difficult to reason with or appeal to the humanity of a person who'd been brainwashed into viewing anyone but a Community flunkey as a threat.

They slunk through the trees and onto the wide stretches of grass in order to make their way to the main house. It was beautiful even in the darkness, with a wraparound porch, clusters of trees hugging the sides, and a single light casting a golden glow on the front. It was so silent and peaceful that Holden had a hard time reconciling it with their mission and everything Six had said.

"You really think they'd keep my mother here?" Holden whispered. "When I spoke to her, I had the impression she was being closely monitored, and this place was lax when I was here."

"She could be, but we'll check both buildings." Six jerked his head at Holden, Nate, and Trent. "You three check the guest house, and me and Lia will go into the main house."

Holden opened his mouth to protest but swallowed it. Lia was far more formidable than he was, and they needed an even distribution of capable humans. When it came down to it, they'd primarily brought Holden along due to his ability to influence people with his talent. Hopefully it didn't come to that point.

"Be careful," Six said, directing it at all of them but staring at Holden. "I'll be pissed if you wind up locked in the silo."

"You and me both."

Holden started to turn to scuttle deeper into the shadows with Nate and Trent, but Six yanked him back for a quick kiss. The energy between them crackled, and Holden felt Six's worry. It'd been so long since anyone had shown true concern for him that he was momentarily at a loss. A search for a witty comment came up empty. Trent rolled his eyes and jerked his shoulder.

"Let's go."

Six nodded and turned away. He and Lia moved together toward the porch and threw themselves over the railing like sleek athletic shadows.

"Let's go," Trent repeated with a note of impatience. "Be moony later."

"I'm not being moony."

Trent didn't respond. Nate had already begun slinking toward the guest house. It was a smaller version of the main, but had less ornamentation and fewer staff members around. There was a guard posted in the front and another standing below the porch steps, but that was it. Six had implied the staff at the Farm were largely unmotivated by their jobs and had no real desire to be isolated in upstate New York, and that seemed to hold true even now. From what Holden saw, the were no additional reinforcements around and nobody seemed particularly tense.

"I don't think anyone saw us coming—psychically or otherwise," Holden said. "But we still need to be careful and not be seen."

"Right," Nate said. "It's too early to get into a back-and-forth with one of them."

"Or to knock someone's head off," Trent added.

Nodding in agreement, Holden scanned the vicinity. "There's a back door leading into the kitchen and two staircases—one going to the attic and the other to the basement. I know this because I used to sneak around looking for booze when I came here as a teen." He jerked his chin toward the yard behind the guest house. "If there's a guard back there too . . ."

"I can try to scale the side," Nate said. "I'm limber."

"I don't know . . ."

"Trust me," Trent said. "He is."

Holden didn't know whether to despise Trent and his deadpan sense of humor at extremely inappropriate times, or to be charmed. No wonder Nate had so ardently resisted Holden last summer.

"No one at the back," Trent said seconds later. "Do you feel anything?"

Nate shook his head, and Holden did the same.

"Stay here," he told Nate. "And try to project some kind of warning if anyone sees you or comes into the house."

"Holden, my empath abilities are still not . . ."

"They're good enough for this. You can do it. I know you can."

Nate was still frowning as he sunk to his knees and disappeared behind the shrubs lining the guest house. Trent lingered before scurrying behind Holden into the back of the house. It was larger than it looked on the outside, but Holden had remembered that from infrequent visits in his youth. The unfocused footprints of his childhood allowed him to take the lead, and guide Trent through a darkened kitchen large enough to cook for a restaurant and through a half hallway serving as a china cabinet. It was untouched, just like it had been years ago, polished enough for moonlight to reflect off the dishes but arranged in a way that would make it cumbersome for anyone to try to use them. Was this all for show? The entire place?

The bottom floor was absent of life except for a woman curled up in a rocking chair in one of the sitting rooms. Holden hadn't noticed her at first, and it was Trent who'd nudged him. Everything from her hair to her eyes had the appearance of having been bleached of color, but she was eerily beautiful and of indistinguishable age. Something about her was familiar, though. Holden stared, frowning, for so long that she turned her head and met his gaze.

Trent stiffened, swearing under his breath, but she didn't do anything else. It was like she didn't actually see them at all.

"Move," Trent hissed. "Before she wakes up from that fog."

Holden didn't have to be told twice. They crept up the stairs with painstaking slowness, and found the master bedroom locked but completely silent. Holden reached out with his gift, and sensed no one on the other side of the door.

The rest of the floor was just as empty as down below. There were two closed doors, but nobody was in the room Holden had once stayed in, and the other bedroom was inhabited by sleeping children who strongly resembled the woman in the rocking chair. Both spaces were large with wood paneling and lots of soft fabrics draping from the windows and covering the beds, but everything was light colored and reeked of a weird perfume.

"Odd," Trent muttered. "Let's get the hell out of here."

They met up with Nate outside, texted Six and Lia that they were moving on, and made the same slow, silent trip to the cottage.

The structure was nearer to the silo than the main and guest houses. Six and Lia were already there, but there was no sign of Holden's mother.

Hunkering down behind the rusted shell of a pickup truck, Holden leaned in. "Did you see Elijah?"

"No. He wouldn't have been there." Six's eyes glittered as he flashed them around the vicinity. "I don't understand why they moved her," he whispered. "Never in all my time here have they kept someone as high profile as her in the cottage."

"Maybe something changed," Lia murmured. "They seem to be getting more paranoid and prone to make stupid-ass decisions if we go by the fact that Richard is no longer above throwing his own son under the bus. Putting Mrs. Payne into a cell could be one more example of that."

Six just kept frowning up at the cottage. It was three levels, made of stucco, and had bars outside the windows. They resembled the white painted security bars you're likely to see on a house in the city rather than a prison, but they still had an ominous quality and contrasted greatly with the opulent decor in the other two buildings.

"She sounded erratic when I spoke to her last," Holden said. "And when we were hanging up, it got more intense. She was frantic to shut me up before I could discuss the situation at Evolution."

Six's frown deepened, but he didn't ask for details. "Let's split up and go inside. There's more security here."

Holden didn't move. He thought about the night they'd confronted Beck, and the way she'd mind controlled Trent into turning on him. It was only a matter of time before they were spotted, and the likelihood of one or more of them being turned into puppets the way Trent had been . . . It made Holden's skin crawl and his stomach churn.

"Six, can you try to extend your shield?" Everyone looked at Holden like he'd lost his mind, including Six, but he persisted. "It's not just about cover of darkness. If someone sees or *senses* us, we're done and everyone will be on high alert."

"I don't know how to do that. It's not possible."

"It is. You've done it to me when we're . . ." Holden glanced at the others, his face heating. Strange how, in the past, he'd talked about sucking dick within days of meeting Nate but referencing the intimacy between him and Six made him antsy. "You've done it before.

Just visualize your shield as if it's a physical object, and then think about it expanding. If you can encompass all of us, that's another layer of protection while we're in the cottage."

"It won't help in the silo," he pointed out. "We'll have to split up, and it's larger."

"I know, but because it's larger, I'm hoping there will be a less concentrated group of guards."

"Good point." Six didn't look sold on being able to use his own shield as protection for the full group, but he jerked his head in a short nod. "I'll give it a shot."

Trent shook his head, likely still thinking this was again starting to resemble a comic book plot. Holden ignored him and covered one of Six's hands with his own. He hoped the strength of their connection would allow Six to spread his invulnerability to the rest of the group.

At first, nothing happened, but then Six's eyes opened wider and Holden saw the psy-kid glow Six had mentioned weeks ago. The glitter brightened the darkness of his eyes, and for a fragment of a second they were as gray as Nate's. It was the most beautiful thing Holden had ever seen, that silvery sheen, before the blanket of protection swept over him. The glow disappeared, but it was replaced by the net of safety. One glance at Lia, Nate, and Trent made it plain they felt the calm force of his power.

Six eased out of his crouch and pulled Holden up with him.

"Let's go."

CHAPTER FIFTEEN

They found her in a bedroom that reeked of flowers. Everything was soft and floral and scented enough for Holden's head to spin as he knelt by his mother's bedside and shook her.

"Mother," he hissed. "Wake up."

There was movement beneath her eyelids and a slight pucker in her brow, but she didn't stir other than that. She was thinner than when he'd last seen her, as if parts of her had faded away until she was vulnerable and small. He feared a harder touch would hurt her fragile body, so he gently shook her again. There was no response.

"What should I do?" he demanded, glancing up at Trent. They'd followed the same plan from the guest house—instructing Nate to wait outside as the rest of them explored the house. "She's not waking up."

"Do some psychic shit," Trent advised, peering into the hallway. "Tickle her with mental fingers or whatever."

"That's not how empathy works."

"Then pour some water on her face, man. Come on. Get with it."

Holden glared at his back before doing a quick scan of the room. It was like a doll's house with barred windows. Not Jessica Payne's style at all. She wasn't one to wrap herself in silks and satins, but she also wasn't one to sleep this deep. In the past, she'd woken up at the slightest creak of a footfall on the stairway. Sneaking out had been impossible. Now she was dead to the world. He'd actually checked her pulse to ensure she was alive.

The vibrating of his phone signaled a text message from Nate. *We have Elijah. Hurry.*

Damn it.

Holden grabbed a half-drunk glass of water sitting next to a pill organizer by her bedside, hesitated only briefly, and then followed Trent's advice. She shot up from bed panting and spluttering with dark hair plastered to her forehead.

"Holden," she slurred, looking at him with eyes that were huge and distant. "What are you doing?"

"I'm getting you out of here."

Holden put his arm around her shoulders and guided her out of bed. He braced for a struggle but instead felt her clinging to his arm as she kicked at the sheets and blankets that had twisted around her feet. He took her black nail polish as a good sign. Parts of her personality were still battling through their attempts to wipe her slate clean. That was made even more apparent when she violently kicked off the blanket and stumbled out of the bed, only to droop in a puddle of a heavy wool nightgown like an extra from *Little House on the Prairie*. Trent hurried over and slid his hand under her other arm.

"Can you walk?"

"The guards," she said, looking around blearily. "Did you kill them?"

Trent did a double take, and Holden could only stare. Part of him had continued to downplay her role in Ex-Comm, but there was no room for that any longer. The woman that had secretly allowed him to stay up watching romantic comedies while they discussed troublesome men and the irritations of love, who'd been a spitfire, sharp teeth beneath pink lipstick and sleek dresses, was apparently capable of killing. Or at least wanting it to be done. She wasn't just his mother. She was the leader of some anti-Community faction, even if she was currently clawing her way to consciousness with great gasping breaths.

He wondered if their brainwashing had ever worked on her, or if it was just drugs that had kept her docile on the phone that day.

"No, Mother, we didn't kill them," he whispered. "So we need to go."

"Yes, let's go." She stepped into a pair of slippers and clung to his arm. "He's coming soon."

"Who?"

"Your father." Jessica shook her head, tawny hair going everywhere. When she stopped, her gaze was clearer, as if she'd spun herself the rest of the way out of a waking dream. "He hasn't been here in a while, and will visit us as soon as he arrives."

"Who's 'us'?" Holden hissed. "You and Chase?"

"No. Me and the other women."

Trent's mouth pulled to the side in a grimace, but he only urged, "We need to move."

They made their way down the dark hallway, only ducking out of sight twice before rejoining the others outside. While encased in the protective shield of Six's mind, it was easier than ever to pinpoint his location inside the barn. Holden had never been inside it before, or any other barn for that matter, but he was certain the barren hayless interior wasn't typical of a working farm. Perhaps the farm had never functioned at all, and it'd been a cover all along.

He barred the door after stepping inside, and made sure his mother took a seat so she could catch her breath. Her head seemed to have cleared during the short adrenaline-fueled flight from the cottage, but her legs were still obviously weak from disuse.

"Holden!"

Elijah's voice was a welcome addition to their little crew. Holden turned just in time to see the drummer flying toward him for a tight hug. He smelled strange, like chemicals instead of sugar and smoke the way he had at the club, but his clutching grip and hitching breaths were familiar.

"I can't believe you're here," he said. "You guys have lost it."

"We can do the reunion thing later," Six said. "We need to start moving out."

"What about Chase?" Elijah demanded, whirling toward Six. "I'm not leaving without him."

"Yes. You are." Six pursed his lips as he peered through a crack at the side of the large barn door. "You and Jessica need to get going now. The bigger this group, the more likely it is that we'll be caught, and the situation has changed."

"My father is here." Holden glanced down at his mother. She'd begun tying her hair in a knot as she sat drowning in the fabric of the enormous nightgown. "Which means he'll have his own security as well."

"Exactly. Time to get the fuck out of here." Six turned just to jerk his chin at Trent. "You good to take Elijah on my bike?"

Trent and Nate exchanged glances, an unspoken communication that lasted for all of ten seconds before Trent inclined his head. For a void who'd been introduced to the Community and the existence of the supernatural only recently, he was handling it shockingly well.

"I'm good to do what I need to do as long as you help Nate find his brother."

Jessica's head popped up at that. Her eyes sharpened on Nate, but she didn't say anything.

Six tossed his keys at Trent's chest. "The best way to get out of here is to go south toward the lake and either take one of the boats across or go the long way and cut across the fie—"

Elijah stood between them with his hands curled into fists. Like Holden's mother, he was lost in oversized white pajamas, and his feet were bare. "I'm not leaving until I know Chase is safe, and you disagreeing with me and treating me like a child is only going to slow us down."

Holden couldn't argue with his reasoning, especially given the shock waves of heartache Elijah was setting off in the barn. Wave after wave of fear and concern bowled Holden over until he wanted to shout at Six to reactivate the goddamn shield, because he'd clearly let it drop at some point.

The grief choked Holden and left no question about Elijah's feelings for Chase. It had always been an unspoken thing between them all at the club, because Elijah was a free spirit who flitted from person to person and did as he pleased. For a time, people had whispered that his affections had been for Holden himself, but either that had never been true or he'd only recently realized he was in love with Chase.

"Okay," he found himself saying. "I understand."

Six shot him an incredulous glare, and Holden arched a brow. Six's mouth sunk at the sides. After a second, he nodded and dismissed Elijah to focus his attention on Jessica.

"How far can you walk?"

"As far as I need to," she said hoarsely. "Are you getting the others out?"

"Just Chase. We're not planned enough for a bigger move right now."

A flicker of regret flashed across her face. "I see. If you're going to retrieve him, now is the time. People are doing supply runs in preparation for Richard's arrival, including Jasper. I don't feel him on the property right now." She stole another glance at Nate before reaching out for Lia. "Help me up, darling."

Lia complied, wrapping an arm around her narrow shoulders. "You ready to ditch all these men?"

"Extremely ready," Jessica croaked. "They'll only slow us down."

Now that sounded like Holden's mother. He wanted to smile, but he still felt like she was a stranger.

"We need to talk soon," he said to her.

"We do. And I'll tell you everything, but right now you all need to go before Richard realizes what's happening. He'll kill you all before he allows this many people to defect. It would create cracks in the Community that he can't privately repair." Jessica's fingers tightened around Lia's upper arm. "He's with the woman in the guest house, and then he'll come to see me. Once he realizes I'm gone, this will go to shit."

"There's no time to find Chase in the silo." Six's scowl was ferocious as he stared at the door again. Holden could see the gears in his head churning out plan after plan before dismissing one after the other. "This is what we're going to do—Lia and Jessica will leave now so we know she's safe, then the rest of you will find Chase and take Holden's vehicle out of here. We'll meet up the road at the bridge, but don't stop before then. There's a police station on 82, but they're under the Community's thumb."

"That's a thing?" Nate asked.

"Of course. Why do you think they want a psychic army? Having the police under their control is only the start of it."

Holden waved his hand, frowning. "Never mind that for now. If we're leaving, what are you going to do?"

Everyone else had seemed to understand this part of the plan except him. Or maybe they were just unwilling to question it.

"Get going," Six said to Lia. "Don't hesitate if they come for you."

Her dark eyes grew larger in her face, but she just offered him a grim nod. "Be careful."

Holden nearly snarled at her to get gone already, and knew how erratic he was being. She was leaving with his mother on a hike that would take at least thirty minutes in her condition, and all he could think was why Six and he were splitting up. His priorities seemed faulty, but then again . . . were they?

Family was turning out to be strings of DNA coded with secrets and lies. His relationship with Six was different. They'd cast aside all the shadowy truths because of the connection between them, and that meant more to him than anything.

He said nothing as Lia and his mother slipped out of the barn without a backward glance, and waited as Elijah led Nate and Trent toward the silo. Nate touched his hand as he left, proving once again that he was an excellent empath despite constantly proclaiming his own failure at the art.

"What's your plan, Six?"

"To distract your father."

Holden stepped forward, grabbing Six's shoulders. "That's ridiculous."

"It's not. When he's done visiting with the woman in the guest house—"

"We need to figure out who she is," Holden said. "She isn't in her right mind. And the kids inside . . ." He shook his head. "I wonder if they're his. If he's been trying to breed psychics as powerful as the Black family. How many families he has like mine, and how many he's destroyed like Nate's and Chase's."

"We might never know that, but I'll throw him off his game before he can check in on your mother." Disgust crossed Six's countenance. It was amazing how long he'd pretended to respect the man he so clearly despised. "I'll tell him I want to come back to the Farm. He'll sit me down and talk about it, try to feel me out with an interrogation since he can't get in my head."

"And you think that will work?"

"Maybe. But if it doesn't, I want you gone before he realizes what's happened." Six lifted his hands to brace Holden's face, rough fingertips gliding over his stubble. "If he finds out that you're involved, everything about your life will change, Holden. You'll lose everything—your apartment, your money, and the club . . ." He trailed off, knowing how much Evolution meant to Holden. "You'll have to give up your old life and go dark. It's what other Ex-Comm people had to do, and it will be even more intense for you and your mother. Richard won't only be betrayed, he'll be humiliated once word gets out. Other members will question why his own wife and son fled. And that will lead to problems. He'll want revenge."

Holden nodded numbly. It was true. It was all true. "Meet us by the pond?"

Six's brow puckered and his mouth opened, but then he looked away and nodded. "Okay."

It wasn't reassuring. Not at all.

Holden jerked Six closer. "I need you to meet us there, Six. I won't leave without you."

"You will if it comes down to it," Six said harshly, looking off to the side again. "You have more to lose than I do."

"That is bullshit. I have *you* to lose, and right now you're everything to me."

Six's gaze snapped back to Holden. The glacial darkness of his eyes glittered in the shadows of the barn, and his breath caught. "Stop saying shit like that or you're going to break me right here in the middle of this half-assed escape plan."

"If I have to break you in order to keep you, I'll do it."

"Fuck."

Six pressed their lips together. Just once and roughly, but it was enough for Holden to dig his psychic hooks in hard enough to wrap himself in Six. There were no flashing lights or thunderbolts marking that he'd found the one unlikely person who was meant to be his, but he knew it. No one else had ever experienced this overwhelming sense of being surrounded by Six—or of knowing the chaotic darkness that battled the sparks of hope and affection in his mind. And no one else had ever made him feel this necessary. This wanted and loved.

"Be careful," Holden said with a ragged edge. "Please."

"*You* be careful. Talk your way out of trouble if you have to. You're good at that."

Holden didn't agree at all, but he sealed the promise with another kiss before forcing himself to turn away.

His jog to the silo was silent, but there was an undercurrent of menace that pinged with every step. He tried to ignore it the way he'd ignored the sinking feeling in his gut the moment Six had headed back to the guest house.

The others had already found a way inside the silo by the time he caught up with them, but there was no chance of duplicating their entry strategy. By the time he was crouched in the darkness off to the side, a guard was standing right in the doorway, and he looked as though he'd be posted there for a while. Holden's options were limited to staying outside and keeping watch, or knocking the guy out. Hand-to-hand combat wasn't his strong suit, but being persuasive was. Especially to large men with soft mouths who looked like they could benefit from the touch of a queer's hands.

These tricks had been fun in the past, but there was nothing thrilling about walking out of his safe spot to approach a man with a gun at his side.

"Hi there," he called before getting too close. "I have a—"

"Where did you come from?" the guard demanded.

"I just arrived with my father." Holden forced an encouraging smile, like he was giving the man the opportunity to redeem himself before acting the fool. "You know . . . Richard Payne."

A healthy dose of skepticism flattened the guard's mouth. "Holden?"

"Yes, that's me. I know it's hard to see me in the dark." Holden sidled closer, cozying up to the guard so his high Payne cheekbones and tawny hair could be seen in the light above the door. He put a hand on the guard's shoulder and felt the nerves crawling over him like a million spiders. "Troublesome gay son of our fearless leader, and a current tagalong since it'd been a while since I've seen my mother and brother."

"Oh, right." Some of the nerves fled as the man latched on to this line of reasoning, but his vibes were still tinged with worry. What would happen if Holden fucked this up? "I know this is shitty, but I have to make sure you have permission to go up."

Holden leaned in closer, arching an eyebrow, and sensed those nerves begin to scatter again. He projected a sense of calm self-assurance and blew them over all those creepy crawling legs. "My father is in the guest house. I don't think it'd be a good time to interrupt him."

Holden moved his hand in a comforting caress, and felt the nerves do barrel rolls into the thrill of attraction. It was times like these where Holden wondered if the attraction was ever real. Did his ability to influence bring out a bolder sense of intrigue and sexual desire . . . or did it create it in someone who had no actual interest? He hated that question, and loved that he didn't have to ask it of himself with Six.

"I just want to check in with my brother," he said softly. "If you want, we don't even have to mention that I was here. That way they won't know you didn't check in."

The guard's eyes darted around. Relief filled him. "Are you sure that's okay with you?"

"Positive." Holden slid his hand from the man's shoulder and up to the side of his neck. "I appreciate this. Maybe we can talk more after your shift?"

"Yes," he said with a throb in his voice.

Was that thirsty response genuine? Anything was possible. Holden was known in the Community to be an accomplished cocksucker, but he was also laying on the vibes pretty thick. In the end, it didn't matter. He smiled.

"I'll be right down, then."

Thankfully the interior of the silo was seemingly deserted. If there were other people guarding the building, he didn't see them, but he also chose to climb the stairs instead of chancing the freight elevator. As he jogged upward, he had the sense of ascending to a blank portal with no way of knowing where it would lead, but then a sharp brightness exploded in his awareness like a flare, and he knew where to go. So much for Nate doubting his own abilities. That signal had held the strength of an empathic Molotov cocktail. The Black psychics were certainly nothing to fuck with. He just hoped Nate had managed to narrow the signal only to him.

He followed the mental tracers up to the top floor and found the rest of the group crowding the narrow hallway in a pool of moonlight. Trent was standing closest to the exit, likely so he could snatch Nate and flee if things didn't go their way, but Nate and Elijah were cautiously inching closer to the figure crouched on the floor.

Chase didn't look like himself. His body was thinner and harder, and his silver eyes were nearly glowing in the shadow of his capsule-like room. He looked between them like an animal trying to find a way out of its cage, and his breath came out in loud gasps.

"What the fuck have they done to him?"

"They probably have him on triple the shit they're doping your mom with," Trent muttered.

"How do you know?"

"I saw the meds in your mother's room. And they had him on a drip, but we detached it."

Smart boy. Figured the engineer would be the first one to pick up samples and evidence.

"Is he dangerous?" Holden asked, flashing back to the night with Beck. To Trent's face vacant like a stranger's. "Or drugged?"

It was Nate who answered as he crouched beside Chase on the floor. "I don't know, but Chase is in there. I can feel him. He's been … sending me visions for months. I thought they were nightmares, but they weren't. I saw this place in my dreams. This hallway and this room. And the man with the cat eyes."

Ice slid down Holden's spine.

Nate continued. "I've been coaxing him out with the weird connection he forged last summer, but he started resisting once he saw Elijah."

"We need to go," Holden said urgently. "We can carry him if necessary. Take the freight elevator, and knock out anyone who stops us." Holden glanced at Trent. "You're the muscle."

"Oh. Great. Because I'm a void?"

"No. Because you're big and can probably fight."

Trent seemed okay with that. He fearlessly stepped forward and reached for Chase, but Chase scooted backward with wilder eyes.

There was no readily jumping up to flee like there had been with Holden's mother. Just naked panic.

"No. Just go," he panted. "Leave."

"Chase—"

"Go, motherfucker! Before Jasper comes."

Jasper with the cat eyes. The very memory of the man made Holden want to vomit.

Elijah breached the space they'd been trying to give Chase and sank to his knees by his side. He showed no hesitation before putting his hands on Chase, one of the most talented psychics Holden had ever seen, who was currently going feral. He bared his teeth when Elijah drew him closer, and skittered backward once those slim arms closed around his tattooed neck. Everything about them contrasted—height, coloring, hair, and demeanor—but Chase froze once their bodies were pressed together.

"I've got you," Elijah whispered. "And I'm not leaving you. They can go, but I'll stay."

"Please." Chase reached up to bury his hands in Elijah's hair. They were clawed as if to yank and pull, but he just clutched the smaller man. "Please leave me here. I can't go."

"You can," Elijah urged.

"No. I can't. Every time I try—I—" Chase shuddered. "I—"

"Keep trying," Elijah pleaded. "So we can get out of here."

"Elijah," Chase said raggedly. "They brought you here for me. As . . . as an incentive. Or a punishment."

Elijah shuddered, but he only held on tighter. "Push through it, Chase. Just like you did when you told me to get out of New York. And when you tried to warn me and Nate. *Please.*"

Chase's body locked up, his eyes squeezing shut and stress lines forming across his brow. It looked like he was fighting an invisible force, or maybe his own brain trying to make him stay on the floor.

"Please get up for me." By now, Elijah's voice was just a whisper. "For us."

Chase opened his eyes again, and this time they were damp. Another pained gasp escaped his mouth, but he struggled to his knees.

"We need to hurry," Holden said. "Please come with us or you're ensuring they'll have their hands on Elijah and will keep a closer watch next time."

Chase cast Nate a furious look, full of scorn and disgust just like the old days. "You shouldn't have brought him here. I thought it was just you, not all of these extra people."

The words stung, but Holden didn't react. It wasn't as though it was a surprise. After all, Chase had trusted a boy he'd never met living across the country rather than the brother he'd been raised with. But then, their upbringing was what had caused so much lack of trust. Holden was the chosen son and Chase had always been the tool.

"We're not leaving you." Elijah leaped to his feet, one small hand gripping Chase's larger one. "We go together or I don't go at all."

"Fuck," Chase hissed, but this time he managed to stagger to his feet. Holden wondered if it was because Elijah was holding on to him so tight and acting as an anchor. "You're a persistent pain in the ass."

"Yeah, but I'm your pain in the ass. So let's get the hell out of here."

Relief swarmed them all as Chase shuffled along with them, even as he refused to allow anyone but Elijah to support him. However, dread struck down the hope of this all ending with the speed of a viper. From across the farm, Holden could feel that Six was in trouble.

CHAPTER SIXTEEN

"**Y**ou can't do this."

Holden evaded Nate's grasping hand. "Yes, I can."

"No, you fucking can't." Chase attempted to draw himself up to his full height but only succeeded in leaning more heavily on Elijah. As physically weak as Chase was, he was still powerful enough to have used his telepathy to get rid of the guard—apparently planting a thought in his head to leave his position and check the cottages. "You didn't drag my raggedy ass out of that silo just to get caught up by yourself."

"I won't get caught, but thank you for that vote of confidence." Holden glanced in the direction of the guest house. "Run south until you hit the lake. There should be a boat you can take to get to the road where Six's bike is, instead of running the whole way with Chase. Leave us the bike and go back up north until you get to my car."

Trent didn't disagree with the plan and quickly swapped keys. His usual jokes and retorts had dried up as the sense of imminent danger cloaked them all. The only thing he exuded was a sense of urgency to get Nate to safety.

"Holden, I don't have a good feeling about this," Elijah said. "Please just—"

"No," he said sharply. "You wouldn't leave Chase. And Nate would never leave Trent. There's no goddamn difference here. I'm not walking away without knowing if he's okay."

Holden could see the questions in Elijah's face, the doubts and surprise that he felt this strongly for a man who had started out as a handler and an assumed spy. But there was no time left to pacify them or explain. And for Holden there were no other options. He would go back, and he would make sure Six was safe. Regardless of the outcome.

"We'll wait for you by the lake for as long as we can," Nate whispered. "Be careful."

Holden nodded once before sprinting away. His speed was reckless, but the urgency he'd felt in Trent was mirrored in himself. Not knowing what was happening was creating an inferno of doubt and terror that churned in his stomach until he felt sick.

He slowed only to duck behind a structure or slink through the shadows when he got too close to guards, but he made it to the guest house in less than a third of the time it'd originally taken them to carefully pick their way to the silo.

There were more people in the area around the main and guest houses, but Holden's senses pinpointed on only two. The commanding force of his father's icy veins, and the wavering blankness of Six. He'd drawn his mental shield up tight. Even Holden had trouble penetrating it, and he could only hope that his father wasn't able to move past it at all.

With the house full of and surrounded by additional security, there was no way to stealthily sneak inside. Barging in the front door would put him in the same position he worried Six was in. Interrogated and holed up with a man who was willing to kill and torture to gain the kind of control he wanted over the Community.

Ignoring the building dread and the doubts that he would be able to save Six if it came down to it, Holden crouched by the side of the house and examined the exterior. There was a balcony on the second level that he could attempt to pull himself up to, but he'd have to access athleticism that had long since been buried in years of drinking, sex, and brisk walks to Broadway to catch cabs. Maybe those months of doing Pilates would come in handy.

Holden uncoiled from his crouch, channeled Six's measured graceful movements, and pulled himself onto the edge of the railing. After a second of wobbling, he pressed his palms against the side of the house and finger-walked them upward until he could grip the bottom rail. Once his hands were securely wrapped around the rails, he pulled himself up with a pained grunt. To hell with Pilates. He needed to go back to upper-body strength training a few times a week.

Sweat trickled down his face and the back of his neck as he awkwardly hauled himself up onto the balcony, nearly falling as he swung himself over the side. He sucked in several deep breaths and prayed no one had heard the clatter of his feet slamming against the floor. The surface of his relief shattered once he realized there was nowhere to go if he was spotted.

Holden hunkered down and crept across the balcony. The sliding door was surprisingly unlocked. It made sense once he realized he was in a room nearly identical to his mother's prison in the cottage—white and pastel colors, floral designs, and the stink of some kind of perfumed spray. If this room belonged to the woman who'd gazed placidly out the window downstairs, Richard likely expected her to be too far gone to attempt a daring escape off the balcony.

The room was empty, and the hallway outside of it was equally deserted. Voices carried from somewhere nearby, but he hesitated to charge toward them without knowing what he would find. Holden searched his memory of the property, and his own time spent in this guest house, and his gaze fell on the double shutters of the closet.

It'd been years since he'd thought about the interconnecting doorway hidden inside, and only his conversations with Six about the property had brought it to the surface of his mind. The interconnecting door opened to a short hallway leading to a matching doorway in the guest house's master suite—the one that had been locked on their first go round.

Voices emanated from that room now, one of which unlocked fight-or-flight instincts in Holden. The sound of his father almost sent Holden spinning away from the doorway because he was too close, and maintaining this proximity was like jumping into a dark pool of water without being able to swim, but he fought the urge to flee.

Six was in there, and that mattered more than his fear.

"—the truth, Sixtus."

"I've told you the truth. I have no desire to keep playing babysitter in Manhattan. The club is fine. Your son is up to nothing. I want my job back, or the equivalent to the one I had here. Maybe a position at the CW location in DC."

Holden knelt on the floor and marveled at the calm in Six's voice.

"You requested to go to the city," Richard said. "You said you wanted off the Farm for a while."

"And I do. But not to waste my time keeping an eye on your son. My talents would be more suited elsewhere considering the most suspicious thing Holden has done in the past month was hole up in his office out of depression when his friend disappeared."

The silence that followed was pointed. Holden wondered why the hell Six would dredge that up, and whether this was a part of his invulnerability. Could he not feel the menace rolling off Richard? Or was his lack of filter the way they'd always gotten along? Either way, Holden inched closer and put his hand next to the doorknob.

"I have reason to believe Elijah Estrella, my son's friend as you put it, is communicating with individuals from Ex-Comm."

"I don't know anything about that."

"I see that, which makes me wonder what you've been doing at Evolution if not noticing the goings-on of individuals at the club."

Six scoffed softly. "All right, Dick. I see where you're going with this, and I'll tell you two things right now. First—Elijah Estrella was barely at the club, and I was never assigned to follow all of Holden's friends. And second—you clearly have this job triple stacked with guys from your security team if you have insight I myself haven't gleaned, so what is the reason for keeping me there?"

"You're right. There's none. But I suspected you'd want to since you've begun fucking my son."

The air rushed out of Holden's lungs so abruptly, he thought they must have heard him gasp. Richard knew. And now Holden had no doubts that this was all fucked. He closed his eyes and prayed for Six not to lie, because that would crush this already crumbling plan to dust.

"How is that relevant?" Six asked dryly. "I still don't want the job."

At that point, Richard did something Holden had never expected—he laughed. "My, oh my, and to think I expected an invulnerable to be immune to his goddamn charms and persuasion. Foolish of me, considering you'd been holed up on the Farm since hitting puberty. And believe me, Six, I know how my son loves to throw himself at men of your stature."

"Men of my stature."

"Yes. I've made an ardent attempt to keep track of my son's many lovers over the years to see if there were any Ex-Comm members taking advantage of his promiscuity. It didn't take long to realize he had a type. Big men who were just discovering their queerness or else who didn't identify as queer at all until Holden unlocked it inside of them with his talent." There was cold amusement behind the words, but Richard's entire aura was throbbing anger. Holden felt it like a thousand white-hot needles flying through his connection and embedding into his soul, and he knew this was a setup. "Would you say that's what happened with you?"

Don't answer, Holden thought at Six, trying hard to project it to him. *Don't let him goad you.*

But it was too late because, unlike him, Six didn't pick up on the cues. He didn't feel the menace.

"Your son doesn't need to influence people to get them to sleep with him."

"No?"

"No," Six said flatly. "I think your son is loyal and incredible, and you'd be better suited treating him as a valuable part of your family than like a brainless idiot who you can use as a scapegoat for your mistakes."

There was a pause in the conversation that prompted Holden to push the door open just a bit so he could peer into the room. The closet was situated in the far corner, and was behind Richard's desk. Holden could see him sitting straight as an iron rod with his hands gripping the arms of his chair. Across the desk from him, Six stared back dispassionately.

"What mistakes would those be, Sixtus?"

"The mistakes you made while trying to find a purpose for the club. Do you remember saying that? That everyone and everything in the Community should have a purpose, and you didn't think a club catering only to queer psychics had enough of one to remain open. But then you heard chatter that the club was attracting psychics from walks of life that didn't usually lead to you and yours, and you sent Beck."

"I sent her to scout untapped talent."

"Yeah, and you took her off a torturing detail here to do it. You knew she was power hungry, and you knew she would gag Chase because he'd recognize her from this place, but you still let her go. Holden didn't have a chance in hell of realizing what she was until it was too late. All because you wanted to use his club as a hunting ground to cherry-pick psychics for your new project. And now you're making him bear your cross and take the blame for letting it all go down."

The anger in Richard had increased to a constant pulse so strong it was starting to become Holden's as well. His own helplessness and fear fell away to great bursts of rage that he'd ever felt helpless or afraid to begin with, and that he was hiding in a closet while this all went on. It was that thought that sent Holden shifting out of the closet in a trench-crawl and brought him closer to Richard's desk. He thought it must be possible for his father to feel him there, present and leeching anger that twined with his own to become an unstoppable magma burst, but then the cool calming shroud of Six's shield enveloped him. And he was free of that concern as well.

"You really have been compromised," Richard said with some astonishment but even more disgust. "My god, my son really knows how to sink his hooks in."

Holden rose to his feet and grabbed the iron disk displayed on Richard's bookcase like a plaque. The same disk his mother had hurled at the wall in a fit of rage so many years ago.

"Are we done with this conversation?" Six asked, fathomless eyes never once shifting behind Richard's shoulder. "Or can we move on to my next assignment?"

"That won't be possible, Six. Not until you receive realignment."

Fear strangled Holden then, because he'd expected this. No matter how Six had believed that Richard had trusted him, it all came down to utility. And once someone stopped being useful to him, or he lost faith in them, it was over. He severed the connection and moved on.

But Holden wasn't going to let him lock Six in a cell. Even if it meant hurting his own father. He'd do what he had to do to get out of here with Six. Alive.

Holden cracked the disk against Richard's temple with enough force to send the man flying from his chair. Immediately after the impact, Holden froze. The disk had been very heavy, and Richard was lying very still. Panic exploded inside of Holden, and he dropped the disk.

"He's fine," Six said. "We need to go before someone finds him or he wakes up and alerts his security team and the guards."

Holden stared down at his father's sprawled body, limp hands, and slack mouth. It was the first time he'd ever seen him vulnerable. The first time his presence hadn't set off a domino effect of anxiety and fear until Holden was flailing to calm himself and cope.

All at once, Holden was a kid again, and he was seeing the fallout of something he'd later repress and put away even though this awful tightness in his chest would sometimes rear up when there were loud sounds or shouting, and he wouldn't remember why.

Or maybe he would remember this moment, because this time, he wasn't going through it alone.

Holden looked up at Six.

"Do you think he'll wake up?"

Six knelt to take Richard's pulse. "Yes."

Holden nodded jerkily and started for the closet again, needing not only to rejoin the others and escape but to get away from his father slumped and sluggishly bleeding on the floor. He thought he should have felt something at the sight, but he didn't. He felt nothing at all. As though all of Richard's rage had burned through him in that one violent motion and left a husk.

"They're waiting for us at the lake."

The Farm was quiet and full of secrets Holden wasn't sure he'd ever learn. He told himself it didn't matter, that he had time to find out more about the drugged children and woman living in the guest house, or why any of that was happening, and ran alongside Six. To safety.

He thought they would make it unmolested, but as they reached the very edge of the property, light flooded everything.

Undoubtedly, Richard had woken up. He might have been a low-rate psychic just like his useless gay son, but he had a presence that whipped out across the acres like silent thunder. The shrill scream of an alarm shattered the stillness of the night.

"Run," Six shouted. "They'll be on bikes!"

On bikes with guns. Just the thought of the two people from the road with their dirt bikes and dark leathers propelled Holden forward. He didn't feel his feet or the breath ripping out of him in whoosh after painful whoosh until their pounding footsteps came to a halt at the edge of the lake. Nate, Trent, Elijah, and the hunched-over figure of Chase were still there, but they'd jumped into action and were pushing one of the boats into the water.

"Let's get the fuck out of here," Trent yelled over the alarms and the distant roar of dirt bikes. "We disabled the other boats!"

They clambered over the side just as Nate started the motor, but it was too late. The two guards from the road skidded to a stop on the embankment in a blur of dark leather and whipping hair. They were eerily similar and both had intense psy-kid eyes.

The boat barely bounced a yard away before one of the guards raised his pistol and fired. The sound boomed through the night like a cannon, deafening and more terrible than anything Holden had ever heard. He expected to be hit, for pain or blood to explode out of his chest, but it was Elijah who cried out and fell backward out of the boat.

A chorus of screamed no's echoed wildly, followed closely by Nate shouting, "Chase, wait—"

It was too late. Chase dove into the water as more shots rang out. He disappeared beneath the freezing-cold water.

CHAPTER SEVENTEEN

The speedboat soared across the lake like a quiet missile bouncing along the cold water.

At some point, Holden had taken over driving the boat. He had more experience on the water, but Six knew more about the area. His low deep voice was soothing as he navigated them away from their originally planned destination and took them southeast toward another town. Holden had feared they would be followed despite Trent's confident claim that he'd made the other two boats unusable, but nobody came for them.

It was quiet and eerie, and the lake was far larger than he'd expected—extending out wide with the other town only a set of twinkling lights in the distance.

"Where are we going?" Nate asked quietly.

"Away from the farm." Six was tense beside Holden, but he glanced back at Nate's pale face before checking himself. "It's safer if we just go rather than returning to the vehicles. We'll ditch the boat farther south and then split up."

"Why do we have to split up?" Holden demanded. "We need to figure out what to do."

"I know." Six wrapped his fingers around the railing and stared out into the water as the wind whipped his hair loose from the knot he'd tied it in. "But if they follow us, and they will, it's better if we're not all traveling together. We can regroup in a bigger city, and tell Jessica and Lia to do the same."

"We could meet up in Poughkeepsie," Trent said. "I have a friend who teaches at Vassar."

"And your friend won't mind hosting runaway psychics?"

"Well, dude, I wouldn't put it to her like that, but I think she'd be cool."

Holden nodded, latching on to that idea with both hands. A plan was good. It was what he needed to feel like all of this wasn't flying apart and floating in different directions until everything was too far out of his reach. "Just so we're clear, we're going to regroup and figure out how to get back to the Farm?"

"Yes. If they're still alive—"

"They are," Nate cut Six off sharply. "At least Chase is. I can feel him."

Holden didn't have to ask why he couldn't feel his half brother. The Payne bond they shared was nothing compared to the Blacks. The power flowing in their veins might have allegedly been borne of generations of inbreeding, but it'd resulted in extremely talented youths. Once upon a time, he would have been bitter about it. Now, he was thankful for the confirmation that Chase's heart was still beating. If only they could say the same for Elijah.

The rest of the boat ride passed in silence. Before he was ready, they were jumping out and onto a muddy embankment in the middle of vast, endless fields. It was a darkness Holden had never seen before, one that was impossible to achieve in New York City. For miles around, there was nothing but fields, crop lines, trees, and the moonlight- and star-filled sky shining down on them.

"You go east," Six told Nate and Trent. "We'll go south, and plan to be in Poughkeepsie by morning. Where in the city are we meeting?"

"Let's say the campus book store at Vassar. Opens at ten."

Six pulled his phone out of his pocket and texted the information to Lia. Immediately after, he dismantled his phone. "They'll be searching for me, so I plan to go on my own. The three of you—"

"Don't try it, Sixtus."

Six's mouth was pressed together so tight it was a slash in his handsome face. "You'd be safer without me."

"That's bullshit," Holden said. "If we're together, we can watch each other's backs." Time to pull out the big guns. "And you can make us both impenetrable."

It was an argument Six couldn't deny. Judging from the way he instantly wrapped Holden in his mental shield, he didn't really want to.

"Vassar's bookstore opens at ten," Trent repeated when nobody else spoke.

"And then we'll figure out our next move," Nate added.

They set out then, two figures—one slim and towheaded and the other brawny and dark haired—trekking across the field with long strides. Holden watched them go and was surprised at how protective he felt of the couple. They hadn't had the most successful interactions in the past, but Nate and Trent's willingness to cross the country and dive back into danger said a lot. They sounded more like Ex-Comm material than Holden did himself.

"Holden."

Turning his gaze away from the steadily decreasing forms, Holden tiredly focused on Six. He looked as exhausted as Holden felt. As though every ounce of his energy had been wrung out into the lake. But it wasn't the physical fatigue that really stood out—it was the dull cloud of defeat hovering around him.

"If you hadn't gone back and distracted him, we would have never gotten Chase far enough to get on that boat."

"But he didn't make it out," Six said hoarsely. "Neither of them did. It was a total goddamn failure."

"You got my mother out. The leader of Ex-Comm." Holden drew Six into an embrace and sighed softly when it was automatically returned. That strong body wrapped around his own and melted. "And you didn't have to go back for them at all. Empathy or no empathy, you're such a fucking good person, Six. You're so goddamn brave."

"So are you."

Holden scoffed. "Right."

Six leaned far enough away to pin Holden with one of his intense I'm-not-taking-your-bullshit stares.

"You have no idea of your worth, Holden. Because you grew up with that fucking monster. And I know you heard what he said."

"It doesn't matter."

"It does matter," Six said sharply. "Because it's bullshit. I knew he was trying to make me angry enough to say the wrong thing and give myself away, but I didn't care. That's the first and the last time I sit by and listen to someone say that shit about you without ending them. Do you understand?"

Holden shrugged, trying to look after Nate again, but Six gripped his chin and kept it immobile. "Say that you understand me," he said urgently. "And that you know how much it means that you came back for me even though you just gave up your entire life."

"I don't care about that. I just wanted you to be safe."

"Exactly. And that's why you should know he's wrong." Six jerked him close enough to kiss. "Precogs in Ex-Comm saw this moment, Holden. They saw you here with me. They knew you would join us, but I wasn't so sure because I don't trust psys the way they do." His face grew fiercer, and his hands gripped tighter. "Premonitions are fickle, and everything you said and did could have changed this outcome. But it didn't. And it had nothing to do with fate. It had to do with you. Only you. Putting yourself at risk for Elijah. And Chase. And for me."

Little by little, the void that had widened inside of Holden began to fill. As that empty coldness was filled with warmth, the connection between him and Six strengthened. Every word cleared Holden's mind, and he could once again feel Six. Just Six. The dark bits that were tangled and gnarled after years of existing in this hateful place, but also other parts of him that were strong and full of hope and love.

It was nothing Holden had ever felt—this absolute tie with another person. There was so much between them that he'd never experienced before and had never expected. More than a burst of lust or anger or sadness that he could hook in to and play with until he milked out a certain response from the person emitting the impression. With Six, he could feel every corner of his mind and cavity of his heart. He knew him better than he'd ever known anyone else.

Holden pulled him into a brief, hard kiss. "The next time we're in a dangerous situation, we're never splitting up again."

"I'll try not to suggest it."

"Just don't, because I refuse to let you out of my sight again."

That tiny grin found its way onto Six's mouth right before he brushed it against Holden's forehead. "Are you ready for this, Holden? Not just getting to Vassar. I'm talking about meeting the rest of

Ex-Comm, coming up with a plan to get onto the Farm and get back Elijah and Chase . . . Everything. Are you sure you don't want to just go back to Evolution and pretend you were never here?"

"I couldn't, even if I wanted to. After everything I saw tonight, there's no way I could go back to that life. I'm not even sure that life was ever real. It all seems so pointless now."

Six slid his hand down to link with Holden's. "It wasn't. You tried your best to make a safe place for people like you, and that mattered. People knew you cared. *I* knew you cared all of those years ago at the tribunal. And, until I met your mother, that one moment with you was the only reason I didn't let myself believe there were only two types of psychics—sheep and the predators."

That was exactly what the Community was starting to look like, though. A hunting ground for predators with agendas he couldn't begin to understand, and a false haven for vulnerable psys who only wanted a place to belong. Besides the urge to rescue his friends, Holden couldn't stop thinking about the rest of it. And he was starting to think about ways to stop it.

"You said Ex-Comm saw me coming?"

"Yes."

"Did they see me taking down the Community? Because that's the only other place to go from here."

"I don't know if they saw that much, but I'm not surprised. Beneath your suits and ties and designer sunglasses, I knew you were a fighter." Six squeezed his hand tighter. "And I loved watching your inner defector grow."

Out of all the compliments Holden had received in his life, that was the best one. Six had believed in him all along. Even before he'd believed in himself.

Six looked into the distance. "Are you ready?"

Holden nodded. "Let's go."

Together they walked away from the lake as the moonlight shone down on them like a promise to guide them to their next destination.

GET READY FOR BOOK THREE OF THE COMMUNITY:

SIGHTLINES

Chase Payne is a walking contradiction. He's the most powerful psychic in the Community, but the least respected. He's the son of the Community's founder, but with his tattoo sleeves and abrasive attitude, he's nothing like his charismatic family. No one knows what to make of him, which is how he wound up locked in a cell on the Farm yet again. But this time, the only man he's ever loved is there too.

Elijah Estrella was used to being the sassy sidekick who fooled around with Chase for fun. But that was before he realized the Community wasn't the haven he'd believed in and Chase was the only person who'd ever truly tried to protect him. Now they're surrounded by people who want to turn them against their friends, and the only way out is to pretend the brainwashing works.

With Chase playing the role of a tyrant's second-in-command, and Elijah acting like Chase's mindless sex toy, they risk everything by plotting a daring escape. In the end, it's only their psychic abilities, fueled by their growing love for each other, that will allow them to take the Community down once and for all.

Dear Reader,

Thank you for reading Santino Hassell's *Oversight*!

We know your time is precious and you have many, many entertainment options, so it means a lot that you've chosen to spend your time reading. We really hope you enjoyed it.

We'd be honored if you'd consider posting a review—good or bad—on sites like **Amazon, Barnes & Noble, Kobo, Goodreads, Twitter, Facebook, Tumblr,** and your blog or website. We'd also be honored if you told your friends and family about this book. Word of mouth is a book's lifeblood!

For more information on upcoming releases, author interviews, blog tours, contests, giveaways, and more, please sign up for our weekly, spam-free newsletter and visit us around the web:

    Newsletter: tinyurl.com/RiptideSignup
    Twitter: twitter.com/RiptideBooks
    Facebook: facebook.com/RiptidePublishing
    Goodreads: tinyurl.com/RiptideOnGoodreads
    Tumblr: riptidepublishing.tumblr.com

Thank you so much for Reading the Rainbow!

RiptidePublishing.com

ACKNOWLEDGMENTS

Thank you everyone who gave me feedback on this project! I get nervous when trying to balance the romance and the suspense, combined with all of the paranormal elements, but early readers—Ashley and Piper in particular—helped a lot with awesome feedback.

Special thanks to the readers who enjoyed *Insight*, and who have been asking for more of The Community! A particularly warm thank-you to BH, Leslie, Candie, Shirlene, Christina, Vinita, Renae, LaCresha, Mirjana, and Sandy! You guys are rock stars.

I appreciate everyone who is along for the ride in my writing journey, especially as I bounce between subgenres. Look out for the last book in this trilogy coming in the fall!

ALSO BY
SANTINO HASSELL

After Midnight
Stygian

The Five Boroughs series
Sutphin Boulevard
Sunset Park
First and First
Interborough
Concourse
Citywide (coming soon)

The Community series
Insight
Sightlines (coming soon)

The Barons
Illegal Contact
Down by Contact

Cyberlove
Strong Signal
Fast Connection
Hard Wired
Mature Content

ABOUT
THE AUTHOR

Santino Hassell was raised by a conservative family, but he was anything but traditional. He grew up to be a smart-mouthed, school-cutting grunge kid, then a transient twentysomething, and eventually transformed into an unlikely romance author.

Santino writes queer romance that is heavily influenced by the gritty, urban landscape of New York City, his belief that human relationships are complex and flawed, and his own life experiences.

Website: santinohassell.com
Facebook: facebook.com/santinohassellbooks
Facebook Group: facebook.com/groups/gethasselled
Newsletter: santinohassell.com/newsletter
Twitter: twitter.com/SantinoHassell
Instagram: instagram.com/santinohassell
Patreon: patreon.com/santinohassell

Enjoy more stories like *Oversight* at RiptidePublishing.com!

Rogue Magic
ISBN: 978-1-62649-528-9

Murder Once Seen
ISBN: 978-1-62649-429-9

Earn Bonus Bucks!

Earn 1 Bonus Buck for each dollar you spend. Find out how at RiptidePublishing.com/news/bonus-bucks.

Win Free Ebooks for a Year!

Pre-order coming soon titles directly through our site and you'll receive one entry into a drawing for a chance to win free books for a year! Get the details at RiptidePublishing.com/contests.

72576454R00130

Made in the USA
Columbia, SC
21 June 2017